THE STORY OF THE BEAUTY AND THE BEAST

The Original Classic French Fairytale

UNABRIDGED EDITION

Story by Madame de Villeneuve
Translated by J. R. Planché
Adapted by Rachel Louise Lawrence

Blackdown*Publications*

This revised edition of Gabrielle-Suzanne Barbot de Villeneuve's "*La Belle et la Bête*" (1740) from 'Four-and-twenty Fairy Tales selected from those of Perrault and other popular writers' (1858), translated by James Robinson Planché, first published in 2014 by Blackdown Publications

Blackdown*Publications*
Address 83 Blackdown View, Ilminster, Somerset TA19 0BD
Email blackdownpublications@mail.com

ISBN-13: 978-1502992970
ISBN-10: 1502992973

Folklore Type: ATU-425C (Beauty and the Beast)

CONTENTS

pirates, all the ships he had at sea; his correspondents made him a bankrupt, his foreign agents were treacherous; in short, from the greatest opulence, he suddenly fell into the most abject poverty. He had nothing left but a small country house, situated in a lonely place, more than a hundred leagues from the city in which he usually resided.

Impelled to seek a place of refuge from noise and tumult, he took his family to this retired spot, who were in despair at such a revolution. The daughters of this unfortunate merchant were especially horrified at the prospect of the life they should have to lead in this dull solitude.

For some time they flattered themselves that, when their father's intention became known, their lovers, who had hitherto sued in vain, would be only too happy to find they were inclined to listen to them. They imagined that the many admirers of each would be all striving to obtain the preference. They thought if they wished only for a husband they would obtain one; but they did not remain very long in such a delightful illusion. They had lost their greatest attractions when, like a flash of lightning, their father's splendid fortune had disappeared, and their time for choosing had departed with it. Their crowd of admirers vanished the moment of their downfall; their beauty was not sufficiently powerful to retain one of them.

Their friends were not more generous than their lovers. From the hour they became poor, every one, without exception, ceased to know them. Some were even cruel enough to impute their misfortunes to their own acts. Those whom the father had most obliged were his most vehement calumniators: they reported that all his calamities were brought on by his own bad conduct, his prodigality, and the foolish extravagance of himself and his children.

This wretched family, therefore, could not do better than depart from a city wherein everybody took a pleasure in insulting them in their misfortunes. Having no resource whatever, they shut themselves up in their country house, situated in the middle of an almost impenetrable forest, and which might well be considered the saddest abode in the world.

What misery they had to endure in this frightful solitude! They were forced to do the hardest work. Not being able to have any one to wait upon them, this unfortunate merchant's sons were compelled to divide the servant's duties amongst them, as well as to exert themselves in every way that people must do who have to earn their livelihood in the country.

The daughters, on their part, had sufficient employment. Like the poor peasant girls, they found themselves obliged to employ their delicate hands in all the labours of a rural life. Wearing nothing but woollen dresses, having nothing to gratify their vanity, existing upon what the land could give them, limited to common necessaries, yet still retaining a refined and dainty taste, these girls incessantly regretted the city and its attractions. The recollection even of their younger days passed so rapidly in a round of mirth and pleasure was their greatest torment.

The youngest girl, however, displayed greater perseverance and firmness in their common misfortune. She bore her lot cheerfully, and with strength of mind much beyond her years: not but what, at first, she was truly melancholy. Alas! Who would not have felt such misfortunes? But, after deploring her father's ruin, could she do better than resume her former gaiety, make up her mind to the position she was placed in, and forget a world which she and her family had found so ungrateful, and the friendship of which she was so fully persuaded was not to be relied upon in the time of adversity?

Anxious to console herself and her brothers by her amiable disposition and sprightliness, there was nothing she did not do to amuse them. The merchant had spared no cost in her education nor in that of her sisters. At this sad period she derived all the advantage from it she desired. As she could play exceedingly well upon various instruments, and sing to them charmingly, she asked her sisters to follow her example, but her cheerfulness and patience only made them more miserable.

These girls, who were so inconsolable in their ill fortune, thought their youngest sister showed a poor and mean spirit, and even silliness, to be so merry in the state it had pleased Providence to reduce them to.

"How happy she is," said the eldest; "she was intended for such coarse occupations. With such low notions, what would she have done in the world?"

Such remarks were unjust. This young person was much more fitted to shine in society than either of them. She was a perfectly beautiful young creature; her good temper rendered her adorable. A generous and tender heart was visible in all her words and actions. Quite as much alive to the reverses that had just overwhelmed her family as either of her sisters; by strength of mind - which is not common in her sex - she concealed her sorrow and rose superior to her misfortunes. So much firmness was considered to be insensibility. But one can easily appeal from a judgment pronounced by jealousy. Every intelligent person, who saw her in her true light, was eager to give her the preference over her sisters.

In the midst of her greatest splendour, although

distinguished by her merit, she was so handsome that she was called "The Beauty". Known by this name only, what more was required to increase the jealousy and hatred of her sisters? Her charms, and the general esteem in which she was held, might have induced her to hope for a much more advantageous establishment than her sisters; but feeling only for her father's misfortunes, far from retarding his departure from a city in which she had enjoyed so much pleasure, she did all she could to expedite it.

This young girl was as contented in their solitude as she had been in the midst of the world. To amuse herself in her hours of relaxation, she would dress her hair with flowers, and, like the shepherdesses of former times, forgetting in a rural life all that had most gratified her in the height of opulence, every day brought to her some new innocent pleasure.

CHAPTER II
THE ENCHANTED PALACE

Two years passed, and the family began to be accustomed to a country life, when a hope of returning prosperity arrived to discompose their tranquillity. The father received news that one of his vessels that he thought was lost had safely arrived in port, richly laden. His informants added, they feared the factors would take advantage of his absence, and sell the cargo at a low price, and by this fraud make a great profit at his expense. He imparted these tidings to his children, who did not doubt for an instant but that they should soon be enabled to return from exile.

The girls, much more impatient than the boys, thinking it was unnecessary to wait for more certain proof, were anxious to set out instantly, and to leave everything behind them. But the father - who was more prudent - begged them to moderate their delight. However important he was to his family at a time when the labours of the field could not be interrupted without great loss, he determined to leave his sons to get in the harvest, and that he would set out upon this long journey.

His daughters, with the exception of the youngest, expected they would soon be restored to their former opulence. They fancied that, even if their father's property would not be considerable enough to settle them in the great metropolis, their native place, he would at least have sufficient for them to live in a less expensive city. They trusted they should find good society there, attract admirers, and profit by the first offer that might be made to them.

Scarcely remembering the troubles they had undergone for the last two years, believing themselves to be already, as by a miracle, removed from poverty into the lap of plenty, they ventured (for retirement had not cured them of the taste for luxury and display) to overwhelm their father with foolish commissions. They requested him to make purchases of jewellery, attire, and headdresses. Each endeavoured to out-vie the other in her demands, so that the sum total of their father's supposed fortune would not have been sufficient to satisfy them.

Beauty, who was not the slave of ambition, and who always acted with prudence, saw directly that if he executed her sisters' commissions, it would be useless for her to ask for anything. But the father, astonished at her silence, said, interrupting his insatiable daughters, "Well, Beauty, do you not desire anything? What shall I bring you? What do you wish for? Speak freely."

"My dear papa," replied the amiable girl, embracing him affectionately, "I wish for one thing more precious than all the ornaments my sisters have asked you for; I have limited my desires to it, and shall be only too happy if they can be fulfilled. It is the gratification of seeing you return in perfect health."

This answer was so unmistakeably disinterested, that it covered the others with shame and confusion. They were so angry, that one of them, answering for the rest, said with bitterness, "This child gives herself great airs, and fancies that she will distinguish herself by these affected heroics. Surely nothing can be more ridiculous."

But the father, touched by her expressions, could not help showing his delight at them. Appreciating, too, the feeling that induced her to ask nothing for herself, he begged she would choose something; and to allay the ill will that his other daughters had towards her, he observed to her that such indifference to dress was not natural at her age that there was a time for everything.

"Very well, my dear father," said she, "since you desire me to make some request, I beg you will bring me a rose; I love that flower passionately, and since I have lived in this desert I have not had the pleasure of seeing one." This was to obey her father, and at the same time to avoid putting him to any expense for her.

At length the day arrived, that this good old man was compelled to leave his family. He travelled as fast as he could to the great city to which the prospect of a new fortune recalled him. But he did not meet with the benefits he had hoped for. His vessel had certainly arrived; but his partners, believing him to be dead, had taken possession of it, and all the cargo had been disposed of. Thus, instead of entering into the full and peaceable possession of that which belonged to him, he was compelled to encounter all sorts of chicanery in the pursuit of his rights. He overcame them, but after more than six months of trouble and expense, he was not any richer than he was before. His debtors had become insolvent, and he could hardly defray his own costs - thus terminated this dream of riches.

To add to his troubles, he was obliged, on the score of economy, to start on his homeward journey at the most inconvenient time, and in the most frightful weather. Exposed on the road to the piercing blasts, he thought he should die with fatigue; but when he found himself within a few miles of his house (which he did not reckon upon leaving for such false hopes, and which Beauty had shown her sense in mistrusting) his strength returned to him. It would be some hours before he could cross the forest; it was late, but he wished to continue his journey.

He was benighted, suffering from intense cold, buried, one might say, in the snow, with his horse; not knowing which way to bend his steps, he thought his last hour had come: no hut in his road, although the forest was filled with them. A tree, hollowed by age, was the best shelter he could find, and only too happy was he to hide himself in it. This tree protecting him from the cold was the means of saving his life; and the horse, a little distance from his master, perceiving another hollow tree, was led by instinct to take shelter in that.

The night, in such a situation, appeared to him to be never-ending; furthermore, he was famished, frightened at the roaring of the wild beasts, that were constantly passing by him. Could he be at peace for an instant? His trouble and anxiety did not end with the night. He had no sooner the pleasure of seeing daylight than his distress was greater. The ground appeared so extraordinarily covered with snow, no road could he find no track was to be seen. It was only after great fatigue and frequent falls that he succeeded in discovering something like a path upon which he could keep his footing.

Proceeding without knowing in which direction, chance led him into the avenue of a beautiful palace, which the snow seemed to have respected. It consisted of four rows of orange-trees, laden with flowers and fruit. Statues were seen here and there, regardless of order or symmetry some were in the middle of the road, others among the trees all after the strangest fashion; they were of the size of life, and had the colour of human beings, in different attitudes, and in various dresses, the greatest number representing warriors.

Arriving at the first courtyard, he perceived a great many more statues. He was suffering so much from cold that he could not stop to examine them. An agate staircase, with balusters of chased gold, first presented itself to his sight: he passed through several magnificently furnished rooms; gentle warmth which he breathed in them renovated him. He needed food; but to whom could he apply? This large and magnificent edifice appeared to be inhabited only by statues. A profound silence reigned throughout it; nevertheless, it had not the air of an old palace that had been deserted. The halls, the rooms, the galleries were all open; no living thing appeared to be in this charming place.

Weary of wandering over this vast dwelling, he stopped in a saloon, wherein was a large fire. Presuming that it was prepared for someone, who would not be long in appearing, he drew near the fireplace to warm himself; but no one came. Seated on a sofa near the fire, a sweet sleep closed his eyelids, and left him no longer in a condition to observe the entrance of anyone. Fatigue induced him to sleep; hunger awoke him; he had been suffering from it for the last twenty-four hours. The exercise that he had taken ever since he had been in this palace increased his appetite. When he awoke and opened his eyes, he was astonished to see a table elegantly laid. A light repast would not have satisfied him; but the viands, magnificently dressed, invited him to eat of everything.

His first care was to utter in a loud voice his thanks to those from whom he had received so much kindness, and he then resolved to wait quietly till it pleased his host to make himself known to him. As fatigue caused him to sleep before his repast, so did the food produce the same effect, and his repose was longer and more powerful; in fact, this second time he slept for at least four hours. Upon awaking, in the place of the first table he saw another of porphyry, upon which some kind hand had set out a collation consisting of cakes, preserved fruits, and liqueurs. This was likewise for his use. Profiting, therefore, by the kindness shown him, he partook of everything that suited his appetite, his taste, and his fancy.

Finding at length no one to speak to, or to inform him whether this palace was inhabited by a man or by a God, fear began to take possession of him, for he was naturally timid. He resolved, therefore, to re-pass through all the apartments, and overwhelm with thanks the Genius to whom he was indebted for so much kindness, and in the most respectful manner solicit him to appear.

All his attentions were useless: no appearance of servants, no result by which he could ascertain that the palace was inhabited. Thinking seriously of what he should do, he began to fancy, for what reason he could not imagine, that some good spirit had made this mansion a present to him, with all the riches that it contained.

This idea seemed like inspiration, and without further delay - making a new inspection of it - he took possession of all the treasures he could find. More than this, he settled in his own mind what share of it he should allow to each of his children, and selected the apartments that would particularly suit them, enjoying the delight beforehand that his journey would afford them. He entered the garden, where, in spite of the severity of the winter, the rarest flowers were exhaling the most delicious perfume in the mildest and purest air. Birds of all kinds blending their songs with the confused noise of the waters, made an agreeable harmony.

The old man, in ecstasies at such wonders, said to himself, "My daughters will not, I think, find it very difficult to accustom themselves to this delicious abode. I cannot believe that they will regret, or that they will prefer the city to this mansion. Let me set out directly," he cried in a transport of joy rather uncommon for him; "I shall increase my happiness in witnessing theirs: I will take possession at once."

Upon entering this charming palace he had taken care, notwithstanding he was nearly perished, to unbridle his horse and let him wend his way to a stable, which he had observed in the forecourt. An alley, ornamented by palisades, formed by rosebushes in full bloom, led to it. He had never seen such lovely roses. Their perfume reminded him that he had promised to give Beauty a rose. He picked one, and was about to gather enough to make half-a-dozen bouquets, when a most frightful noise made him turn round.

He was terribly alarmed upon perceiving at his side a horrible beast, which, with an air of fury, laid upon his neck a kind of trunk, resembling an elephant's, and said, with a terrific voice, "Who gave you permission to gather my roses? Is it not enough that I kindly allowed you to remain in my palace? Instead of feeling grateful, rash man, I find you stealing my flowers! Your insolence shall not remain unpunished."

The good man, already too much overpowered by the unexpected appearance of this Beast, thought he should die of fright at these words, and quickly throwing away the fatal rose. "Ah! My Lord," he said, prostrating himself before the Beast, "have mercy on me! I am not ungrateful! Penetrated by all your kindness, I did not imagine that so slight a liberty could possibly have offended you."

The Beast very angrily replied, "Hold your tongue, you

foolish talker. I care not for your flattery nor for the titles you bestow on me. I am not your Lord; I am The Beast; and you shall not escape the death you deserve."

The merchant, dismayed at so cruel a sentence, and thinking that submission was the only means to preserve his life, said, in a truly affecting manner, that the rose he had dared to take was for one of his daughters, called Beauty. Then, whether he hoped to escape from death or to induce his enemy to feel for him, he related to him all his misfortunes.

He told him the object of his journey, and did not omit to dwell on the little present he was bound to give Beauty; adding that was the only thing she had asked for, while the riches of a King would hardly have sufficed to satisfy the wishes of his other daughters. And so came to the opportunity which had offered itself to satisfy the modest desire of Beauty and his belief that he could have done so without any unpleasant consequences; asking pardon, moreover, for his involuntary fault.

The Beast considered for a moment, then, speaking in a milder tone, he said to him, "I will pardon you, but upon condition that you will give me one of your daughters. I require someone to repair this fault."

"Just Heaven!" replied the merchant. "How can I keep my word? Could I be so inhuman as to save my own life at the expense of one of my children's? Under what pretext could I bring her here?"

"There must be no pretext," interrupted the Beast. "I expect that whichever daughter you bring here she will come willingly, or I will not have either of them. Go, see if there be not one amongst them sufficiently courageous, and loving you enough, to sacrifice herself to save your life. You appear to be an honest man. Give me your word of honour to return in a month. If you cannot decide to bring one of them back with you, she will remain here and you will return home. If you cannot do so, promise me to return here alone after bidding them farewell forever, for you will belong to me. Do not fancy," continued the Beast, grinding his teeth, "that by merely agreeing to my proposition you will be saved. I warn you, if you think so to escape me I will seek you and destroy you and your race, although a hundred thousand men may appear to defend you."

The good man, although quite convinced that he should vainly put to the proof the devotion of his daughters, accepted, nevertheless, the Beast's proposition. He promised to return to him at the time named, and give himself up to his sad fate, without rendering it necessary for the Beast to seek for him.

After this assurance, he thought himself at liberty to retire and take leave of the Beast, whose presence was most distressing to him. The respite was but brief, yet he feared he might revoke it. He expressed his anxiety to depart; but the Beast told him he should not do so till the following day.

"You will find," he said, "a horse ready at break of day. He will carry you home quickly. *Adieu.* Go to supper and await my orders."

The poor man, more dead than alive, returned to the saloon in which he had feasted so heartily. Before a large fire, his supper, already laid, invited him to sit and enjoy it. The delicacy and richness of the dishes had no longer, however, any temptation for him.

Overwhelmed by his grief, he would not have seated himself at the table, but that he feared that the Beast was concealed somewhere, and observing him, and that he would excite his anger by any slight of his bounty. To avoid further disaster, he made a momentary truce with his grief, and, as well as his afflicted heart would permit, he tasted, in turn, the various dishes.

At the end of the repast, a great noise was heard in the adjoining apartment, and he did not doubt that it was his formidable host. As he could not manage to avoid his presence, he tried to recover from the alarm, which this sudden noise had caused him. At the same moment, the Beast, who appeared, asked him abruptly if he had made a good supper. The good man replied, in a modest and timid tone that he had, thanks to his attention, eaten heartily.

"Promise me," replied the Beast, "to remember your word to me, and to keep it as a man of honour, in bringing me one of your daughters."

The old man, who was not much entertained with this conversation, swore to him that he would fulfil what he had promised, and return in a month alone or with one of his daughters, if he should find one who loved him sufficiently to follow him on the conditions he must propose to her.

"I warn you again," said the Beast, "to take care not to deceive her as to the sacrifice which you must exact from her, or the danger she will incur. Paint to her my face such as it is. Let her know what she is about to do: above all, let her be firm in her resolution. There will be no time for reflection when you shall have brought her here. There must be no drawing back: you will be equally lost, without obtaining for her the liberty to return."

The merchant, who was overcome at this discourse, iterated his promise to conform to all that was prescribed to him. The Beast, satisfied with his answer, ordered him to retire to rest, and not to rise till he should see the sun, and hear a golden bell.

"You will breakfast before setting out," he said again, "and you may take a rose with you for Beauty. The horse which shall bear you will be ready in the courtyard. I reckon on seeing you again in a month, if you are an honest man. If you fail in your word, I shall pay you a visit."

The good man, for fear of prolonging a conversation already too painful to him, made a profound reverence to the Beast - who told him again not to be anxious respecting the road by which he should return as, at the time appointed, the same horse, which he would mount the next morning, would be found at his gate and would suffice for his daughter and himself.

However little disposition the old man felt for sleep, he dared not disobey the orders he had received. Obliged to lie down, he did not rise till the sun began to illumine the chamber. His breakfast was soon despatched, and he then descended into the garden to gather the rose, which the Beast had ordered him to take to Beauty.

How many tears this flower caused him to shed. But the fear of drawing on himself new disasters made him constrain his feelings, and he went, without further delay, in search of the horse which had been promised him. He found on the saddle a light but warm cloak. As soon as the horse felt him on his back, he set off with incredible speed.

The merchant, who in a moment lost sight of this fatal palace, experienced as great a sensation of joy as he had on the previous evening felt in perceiving it, with this difference, that the delight of leaving it was embittered by the cruel necessity of returning to it.

"To what have I pledged myself?" said he, whilst his courser carried him with a velocity and a lightness, which is only known in Fairyland. "Would it not be better that I should become at once the victim of this Beast who thirsts for the blood of my family? By a promise I have made, as unnatural as it is indiscreet, I have prolonged my life. Is it possible that I could think of extending my days at the expense of those of my daughters? Can I have the barbarity to lead one to him, to see him, no doubt, devour her before my eyes?

But all at once, interrupting himself, he cried, "Miserable wretch that I am, what have I to fear? If I could find it in my heart to silence the voice of nature, would it depend on me to commit this cowardly act? She must know her fate and consent to it. I see no chance that she will be inclined to sacrifice herself for an inhuman father, and I ought not to make such a proposition to her. It is unjust.

"But even if the affection which they all entertain for me should induce one to devote herself, would not a single glance at the Beast destroy her constancy, and I could not complain. Ah! Too imperious Beast," he exclaimed, "you have done this expressly! By putting an impossible condition to the means, you offer me to escape your fury - and obtain the pardon of a trifling fault - you have added insult to injury!

"But," he continued, "I cannot bear to think of it. I hesitate no longer; and I would rather expose myself without turning away from your rage, than attempt a useless mode of escape, which my paternal love trembles to employ. Let me retrace," he said, "the road to this frightful palace, and without deigning to purchase so dearly the remnant of a life which can never be but miserable without waiting for the month which is accorded me to expire, return, and terminate this day my miserable existence!"

At these words, he endeavoured to retrace his steps, but he found it impossible to turn the bridle of his horse. Allowing himself, therefore, against his will, to be carried forward, he resolved at least to propose nothing to his daughters.

CHAPTER III
BEAUTY'S SACRIFICE

The merchant saw his house in the distance, and strengthening himself more and more in his resolution, "I will not speak to them," he said, "of the danger which threatens me. I shall have the pleasure of embracing them once more; I shall give them my last advice; I will beg them to live on good terms with their brothers, whom I shall also implore not to abandon them."

In the midst of this reverie, he reached his door. His own horse, which had found its way home the previous evening, had alarmed his family. His sons, dispersed in the forest, had sought him in every direction; and his daughters, in their impatience to hear some tidings of him, were at the door, in order to obtain the earliest intelligence. As he was mounted on a magnificent steed, and wrapped in a rich cloak, they did not recognise him, but took him at first for a messenger sent by him, and the rose, which they perceived attached to the pummel of the saddle, made them perfectly easy on his account.

When this afflicted father, however, approached nearer, they recognised him, and thought only of evincing their satisfaction at seeing him return in good health. But the sadness depicted in his face, and his eyes filled with tears, which he vainly endeavoured to restrain, changed their joy into anxiety. All hastened to inquire the cause of his trouble. He made no reply but by saying to Beauty, as he presented her with the rose, "There is what you have demanded of me, but you will pay dearly for it, as well as the others."

"I was certain," exclaimed the eldest, "and I was saying, this very moment, that she would be the only one whose commission you would execute. At this time of the year, a rose must have cost more than you would have had to pay for us all five together; and, judging from appearances, the rose will be faded before the day is ended: never mind, however, you were determined to gratify the fortunate Beauty at any price."

"It is true," replied the father, mournfully, "that this rose has cost me dear, and more dear than all the ornaments which you wished for would have done. It is not in money, however, and would to Heaven that I might have purchased it with all I am yet worth in the world."

These words excited the curiosity of his children, and dispelled the resolution that he had taken not to reveal his adventure. He informed them of the ill success of his journey, the trouble that he had undergone in running after a wildly fanciful fortune, and all that had taken place in the palace of the Beast. After this explanation, despair took the place of hope and of joy.

The daughters seeing all their projects annihilated by this thunderbolt, uttered fearful cries; the brothers, more courageous, said resolutely that they would not suffer their father to return to this frightful palace; that they were bold enough to deliver the earth from this horrible Beast, even supposing he should have the temerity to come in search of him. The good man, although moved at their affliction, forbad them to commit violence, telling them, that as he had given his word, he would kill himself rather than fail to keep it.

Notwithstanding this, they sought for expedients to save his life; the young men, full of courage and filial affection, proposed that one of them should go and offer himself as a victim to the wrath of the Beast; but the Beast had said positively and explicitly that he would have one of the daughters, and not one of the sons. The brave brothers grieved that their good intentions could not be acted upon, and then did what they could to inspire their sisters with the same sentiments. But their jealousy of Beauty was sufficient to raise an invincible obstacle to such heroic action.

"It is not just," they said, "that we should perish in so frightful a manner for a fault of which we are not guilty. It would be to render us victims to Beauty, to whom they would be very glad to sacrifice us; but duty does not require such a sacrifice. Here is the fruit of the moderation and perpetual preaching of this unhappy girl!

"Why did she not ask, like us, for a good stock of clothes and jewels? If we have not had them, it has at all events cost nothing for asking, and we have no cause to reproach ourselves for having exposed the life of our father by indiscreet demands. If, by an affected disinterestedness, she had not sought to distinguish herself, as she is in all things more favoured than we, he would have, no doubt, found enough money to content her. But she must needs, by her singular caprice, bring on us all this misfortune. It is she who has caused it and they wish us to pay the penalty. We will not be her dupe. She has brought it on herself, and she must find the remedy."

Beauty, whose grief had almost deprived her of consciousness, suppressing her sobs and sighs, said to her sisters, "I am the cause of this misfortune; it is I alone who must repair it. I confess it would be unjust to allow you to suffer for my fault. Alas! It was, notwithstanding, an innocent wish. Could I foresee that the desire to have a rose when we were in the middle of summer would be punished so cruelly?

"The fault is committed, however; whether I am innocent or guilty, it is just that I should expiate it. It cannot be attributed to anyone else. I will risk my life," she pursued, in a firm tone, "to release my father from his fatal engagement. I will go to find the Beast; too happy in being able to die in order to preserve the life of him from whom I received mine, and to silence your murmurs. Do not fear that anything can turn me from my purpose; but I pray you, during this month, to do me the favour to spare me your reproaches."

So much firmness in a girl of her age surprised them all much; and the brothers, who loved her tenderly, were moved at her resolution. They paid her infinite attention, and felt the loss they were about to sustain. But it was requisite to save the life of a father. This pious motive closed their mouths and well persuaded that it was a thing decided on. Far from thinking of combating so generous a purpose, they contented themselves by shedding tears, and giving their sister all the praise which her noble resolution merited, all the more from her being only sixteen years of age, and having the right to regret a life which she was about to sacrifice in so cruel a manner.

The father alone would not consent to the design of his youngest daughter; but the others reproached him insolently with the charge that Beauty alone was cared for by him, in spite of the misfortune which she had caused, and that he was sorry that it was not one of the elders who should pay for her imprudence.

This unjust language forced him to desist; besides, Beauty assured him that if he would not accept the exchange, she would make it in spite of him, for she would go alone to seek the Beast, and so perish without saving him. "How do we know," said she, forcing herself to assume more tranquillity than she really felt, "perhaps the dreadful fate which appears to await me conceals another as happy as this seems terrible?"

Her sisters, hearing her speak thus, smiled maliciously at the wild idea; they were enchanted at the delusion in which they believed her to be indulging. But the old man, conquered by all her reasons, and remembering an ancient prediction, by which he had learnt that this daughter should save his life, and that she should be a source of happiness to all her family, ceased to oppose the will of Beauty.

Insensibly, they began to speak of their departure as a thing almost indifferent. It was she who gave the tone to the conversation, and in their presence she appeared to consider it as a happy event; it was only, however, to console her father and brothers, and not to alarm them more than necessary. Although discontented with the conduct of her sisters towards her, who appeared even impatient to see her depart, and thought the month passed too slowly, she had the generosity to divide all her little property and the jewels, which she had at her own disposal amongst them.

They received with pleasure this new proof of her generosity, but without abating their hatred of her. An extreme joy took possession of their hearts when they heard the horse neigh, which was sent to carry away a sister whose amiability their jealous natures would not allow them to perceive. The father and the sons alone were so afflicted that they could not contain themselves at this fatal moment. They proposed to strangle the horse.

Beauty, however - preserving all her tranquillity - showed them again the absurdity of such a design and the impossibility of executing it. After having taken leave of her brothers, she embraced her hardhearted sisters, taking such a tender farewell of them that she drew from them some tears, and they believed, for the space of a few minutes, that they were almost as much afflicted as their brothers.

During these brief, yet lingering leave-takings, the good man, hurried by his daughter, had mounted his horse. She placed herself behind him with as much alacrity as though she were going to make an agreeable journey. The animal rather flew than walked. But this extreme speed did not inconvenience her in the least; the paces of this singular horse were so gentle that Beauty felt no more shaken by him than she would have been by the breath of a zephyr.

In vain, during the journey, her father offered a hundred times to allow her to dismount, and to go himself alone to find the Beast. "Consider, my dear child," he said; "there is still time. This Beast is more terrible than you can imagine. However firm your resolution may be, I cannot but fear it will fail on beholding him; then it will be too late; you will be lost, and we shall both perish together."

"If I went," replied Beauty, "to seek this terrible Beast with the hope of being happy, it is not impossible that that hope would fail me at the sight of him; but as I reckon on a speedy death, and believe it to be unavoidable, what does it signify whether he who shall destroy me be agreeable or hideous."

Conversing thus, night closed around them, but the horse went quite as fast in the darkness. It was, however, suddenly dissipated by a most unexpected spectacle. This was caused by the discharge of all kinds of beautiful fireworks flowerpots, Catherine wheels, suns, bouquets, which dazzled the eyes of our travellers. This agreeable and unlooked-for illumination lighted up the entire forest, and diffused a gentle heat through the air, which was desirable, for the cold in this country was more keenly felt in the night than by day.

By this charming light the father and daughter found themselves in an avenue of orange-trees. At the moment that they entered it, the fireworks ceased. The illumination was, however, continued by all the statues having in their hands lighted torches. Besides these, lamps without number covered the front of the palace, symmetrically arranged in forms of true-lover's knots and crowned ciphers, consisting of double LL's and double BB's. On entering the court they were received by a salute of artillery, which, added to the sound of a thousand instruments of various kinds, some soft some warlike, had a fine effect.

"The Beast must be very hungry indeed," said Beauty, half-jestingly, "to make such grand rejoicings at the arrival of his prey." However, in spite of her agitation at the approach of an event which - according to all appearance - was about to be fatal to her, she could not avoid paying attention to the magnificent objects which succeeded each other and presented to her view the most beautiful spectacle she had ever seen, nor help saying to her father that the preparations for her death were more brilliant than the bridal pomp of the greatest King in the world.

The horse stopped at the foot of the flight of steps. She alighted quickly, and her father, as soon as he had put foot to the ground, conducted her by a vestibule to the saloon in which he had been so well entertained. They found there a large fire, lighted candles, which emitted an exquisite perfume, and, above all, a table splendidly served. The good man, accustomed to the manner in which the Beast regaled his guests, told his daughter that this repast was intended for them, and that they were at liberty to avail themselves of it.

Beauty made no difficulty, well persuaded that it would not hasten her death. On the contrary, she imagined that it would make known to the Beast the little repugnance she had felt in coming to see him. She hoped that her frankness might be capable of softening him, and even that her adventure might be less sad than she had at first apprehended. The formidable Beast with which she had been menaced did not show himself, and the whole palace spoke of joy and magnificence. It appeared that her arrival had caused these demonstrations, and it did not seem probable that they could have been designed for a funeral ceremony.

Her hope did not last long, however. The Beast made himself heard. A frightful noise, caused by the enormous weight of his body, by the terrible clank of his scales, and an awful roaring, announced his arrival. Terror took possession of Beauty. The old man, embracing his daughter, uttered piercing cries. But recovering herself in a moment, she suppressed her agitation. Seeing the Beast approach - whom she could not behold without a shudder - she advanced with a firm step and, with a modest air, saluted him very respectfully.

This behaviour pleased the Beast. After having contemplated her, he said to the old man, in a tone which, without being one of anger, might, however, fill with terror the boldest heart, "Good evening, my good friend." Turning to Beauty, he said also to her, "Good evening, Beauty."

The old man, fearing every instant that something awful would happen to his daughter, had not the strength to reply, but Beauty - without agitation and in a sweet and firm voice - said, "Good evening, Beast."

"Do you come here voluntarily?" inquired the Beast; "and will you consent to let your father depart without following him?" Beauty replied that she had no other intention. "Ah! And what do you think will become of you after his departure?"

"What it may please you," said she; "my life is at your disposal, and I submit blindly to the fate which you may doom me to."

"I am satisfied with your submission," replied the Beast; "and as it appears that they have not brought you here by force, you shall remain with me. As for you, good man," said he to the merchant, "you shall depart tomorrow, at daybreak; the bell will warn you; delay not after your breakfast; the same horse will re-conduct you. But," he added, "when you shall be in the midst of your family, dream not of revisiting my palace and remember it is forbidden you forever.

"You, Beauty," continued the Beast, addressing her, "conduct your father into the adjoining wardrobe, and choose anything which both of you think will give pleasure to your brothers and sisters. You will find two trunks - fill them. It is right that you should send them something of sufficient value to oblige them to remember you."

In spite of the liberality of the Beast, the approaching departure of her father sensibly affected Beauty, and caused her extreme grief; however, she determined to obey the Beast, who quitted them, after having said, as he had done on entering, "Goodnight, Beauty. Goodnight, good man."

When they were alone, the good man, embracing his daughter, wept without ceasing. The idea of leaving her with the Beast was a most cruel trial to him. He repented having brought her into that place. The gates were open; he wished to lead her away again, but Beauty impressed upon him the danger and consequences of such a proceeding.

They entered the wardrobe which had been indicated to them; they were surprised at the treasures it contained. It was filled with apparel so superb that a Queen could not wish for anything more beautiful, or in better taste. Never was warehouse better filled.

When Beauty had chosen the dresses she thought the most suitable, not to the present situation of the family, but proportioned to the riches and liberality of the Beast, who was the donor, she opened a press, the door of which was of rock crystal, mounted in gold.

Although such a magnificent exterior prepared her to find it contain some rare and precious treasures, she saw such a mass of jewels of all kinds, that her eyes could hardly support the brilliancy of them. Beauty, from a feeling of obedience, took without hesitation, a prodigious quantity, which she divided as well as she could amongst the lots she had already made.

On opening the last cabinet, which was no less than a cabinet filled with pieces of gold, she changed her mind. "I think," said she to her father, "that it will be better to empty these trunks, and to fill them with coin, which you can give to your children according to your pleasure. By this means you will not be obliged to confide your secret to anyone, and your riches will be possessed by you without danger. The advantage that you would derive from the possession of these jewels, although their value might be more considerable, would be attended by inconvenience. In order to profit by them you would be forced to sell them, and to trust them to persons who would only look on you with envious eyes.

"Your confidence in them might even prove fatal to you, whilst gold pieces of current coin will place you," she continued, "beyond the reach of any misfortune, by giving you the means of acquiring land and houses, and purchasing rich furniture, ornaments, and precious stones."

The father approved her forethought. But wishing to take for his daughters some dresses and ornaments, in order to make room for them as well as the gold, he took out of the trunks that he had selected for his own use. The great quantity of coin which he put in did not fill them, however. They were composed of folds, which stretched at pleasure. He found room for the jewels, which he had displaced, and, in fact, these trunks contained more than he could even wish for.

"So much money," he said to his daughter, "will place me in a position to sell my jewels at my own convenience. Following your counsel, I will hide my wealth from the world, and even from my children. If they knew me to be as rich as I shall be, they would torment me to abandon my country life, which is the sole one wherein I have found happiness and not experienced the perfidy of false friends with whom the world is filled."

But the trunks were so immensely heavy, that an elephant would have sunk under their weight, and the hope which he had begun to cherish appeared to him a dream, and nothing more. "The Beast mocks us," he said, "and feigns to give me wealth, which he makes it impossible for me to carry away."

"Suspend your judgment," Beauty replied; "you have not provoked his liberality by any indiscreet request nor by any greedy or interested looks. Ridicule would be without point. I think, as the Beast has bestowed it on you, that he will certainly find the means of allowing you to enjoy it. We have only to close the trunks, and leave them here. No doubt he knows by what coach to send them."

Nothing could be more prudent than this advice. The good man, conformably to it, re-entered the saloon with his daughter. Seated together on the sofa, they saw the breakfast instantly served. The father ate with more appetite than he had done the preceding night. That which had come to pass had diminished his despair and revived his confidence.

He would have departed without concern if the Beast had not had the cruelty to make him understand that he must not dream of seeing his palace again, and that he must wish his daughter an eternal farewell. There is no evil but death without remedy. The good man was not completely stunned by this order. He flattered himself that it would not be irrevocable, and this hope prepared him to quit his host with tolerable satisfaction.

Beauty was not so well satisfied. Little persuaded that a happy future was prepared for her, she feared that the rich presents with which the Beast loaded her family was but the price of her life and that he would devour her immediately that he should be alone with her, or at least that a perpetual prison would be her fate and that her only companion would be this frightful Beast.

This reflection plunged her into a profound reverie, but a second stroke of the bell warned them that it was time to separate. They descended into the court, where the father found two horses, the one loaded with the two trunks, and the other destined for himself. The latter, covered with a good cloak, and the saddle having two bags attached to it full of refreshments, was the same that he had ridden before.

So much attention on the part of the Beast again supplied them with subject of conversation; but the horses, neighing and stamping with their hoofs, made known to them that it was time to part.

The merchant, afraid of irritating the Beast by his delay, bade his daughter an eternal farewell. The two horses set off faster than the wind, and Beauty instantly lost sight of them. She mounted in tears to the chamber, which was appropriated to her, where for some time she was lost in sad reflections.

CHAPTER IV
DREAMS

At length, being overcome with sleep, Beauty felt a wish to seek repose, which, during a month past, she had not enjoyed. Having nothing better to do, she was about to go to bed, when she perceived on the table a service of chocolate prepared. She took it, half-asleep, and her eyes almost immediately closed. She fell into a quiet slumber, which since the moment she had received the fatal rose had been unknown to her.

During her sleep, she dreamt that she was on the bank of a canal - a long way off - the two sides of which were ornamented with two rows of orange trees and flowering myrtles of immense size, where, engrossed with her sad situation, she lamented the misfortune that condemned her to pass her days in this place without hope of ever leaving it.

A young man, beautiful as Cupid is painted, in a voice which touched her heart, then said, "Do not, Beauty, believe you will be as unhappy as it now appears to you. It is in this place that you will receive the recompense, which they have elsewhere unjustly denied you. Let your penetration assist you to extricate me from the appearance which disguises me. Judge in seeing me, if my company is contemptible and ought not to be preferred to a family unworthy of you. Wish and all your desires shall be fulfilled. I love you tenderly; you alone can bestow happiness on me by being happy yourself. Never deny me this. Excelling all other women as far in the qualities of your mind as you excel them in beauty, we shall be perfectly happy together."

This charming apparition, then kneeling at her feet, made her the most flattering promises in the most tender language. He pressed her in the warmest terms to consent to his happiness, and assured her that she should be entirely her own mistress.

"What can I do?" said she to him with eagerness.

"Follow the first impulse of gratitude," said he. "Judge not by your own eyes and, above all, abandon me not, but release me from the terrible torment which I endure."

After this first dream, she fancied she was in a magnificent cabinet with a lady whose majestic demeanour and surprising beauty created in her heart a feeling of profound respect. This lady said to her in an affectionate tone, "Charming Beauty, regret not that you have left; a more illustrious fate awaits you; but if you would deserve it, beware of allowing yourself to be prejudiced by appearances."

Her sleep lasted more than five hours, during which time she saw the young man in a hundred different places, and under a hundred different circumstances. Sometimes he offered her a fine entertainment; sometimes he made the most tender protestations to her. How pleasant her sleep was! She would have wished to prolong it, but her eyes, open to the light, could not be induced to close again, and Beauty believed she had only had an agreeable dream.

A clock struck twelve, repeating twelve times her own name, which obliged her to rise. She then saw a toilet-table covered with everything necessary for a lady. After having dressed herself with a feeling of pleasure of which she did not imagine the cause, she passed into the saloon, where her dinner was served.

When one eats alone, a repast is very soon over. On returning to her chamber, she threw herself on the sofa; the young man of whom she had dreamt again presented himself to her thoughts. *'I can make you happy,' were his words. Probably this horrible Beast, who appears to command all here, keeps him in prison. How can he be extricated? He repeated to me that I was not to be deceived by appearances. I understand nothing; but how foolish I am! I amuse myself by seeking for reasons to explain an illusion formed by sleep, and which my waking has destroyed. I ought not to pay attention to it. I must only occupy myself with my present fate, and seek such amusements as will prevent my being overcome by melancholy.*

Shortly afterwards she began to wander through the numerous apartments of the palace. She was enchanted with them, having never seen anything so beautiful. The first that she entered was a large cabinet of mirrors. She saw herself reflected on all sides. At length a bracelet, suspended to a girandole, caught her sight. She found on it the portrait of the handsome Cavalier, just as she had seen him in her sleep.

How was it she recognised him immediately? His features were already too deeply impressed on her mind and perhaps in her heart. With joyful haste, she placed the bracelet on her arm, without reflecting whether this action was correct.

From this cabinet, having passed into a gallery full of pictures, she there found the same portrait the size of life, which appeared to regard her with such tender attention, that she coloured, as if this picture had been the person himself; or that she had had witnesses of her thoughts.

Continuing her walk, she found herself in a saloon filled with different kinds of instruments. Knowing how to play on almost all, she tried several, preferring the harpsichord to the others, because it was a better accompaniment for the voice.

From this saloon, she entered another gallery, corresponding to that in which were the paintings. It contained an immense library. She liked reading and, since her sojourn in the country, she had been deprived of this pleasure. Her father, by the confusion of his affairs, had found himself obliged to sell his books. Her great taste for study could easily be satisfied in this place, and would guarantee her against the dullness consequent on solitude.

The day passed before she could see everything. At the approach of night, all the apartments were illuminated by perfumed wax-lights, placed in lustres either transparent or of different colours, and not of crystal, but made of diamonds and rubies.

At the usual hour, Beauty found her supper served, with the same delicacy and neatness as before. No human figure presented itself to her view; her father had told her she would be alone. This solitude began no longer to trouble her, when the Beast made himself heard. Never having yet found herself alone with him, ignorant how this interview would pass off, fearing even that he only came to devour her, is it any wonder that she trembled?

But on the arrival of the Beast, whose approach was by no means furious, her fears were dissipated. This monstrous giant said, roughly, "Good evening, Beauty." She returned his salutation in the same terms, with a calm air, but a little tremulously. Amongst the different questions that the Beast put to her, he asked how she amused herself.

Beauty replied, "I have passed the day in inspecting your palace, but it is so vast that I have not had time to see all the apartments, and the beauties which it contains."

The Beast asked her, "Do you think you can get accustomed to living here?"

The girl replied, politely, that she could live without trouble in so beautiful an abode.

After an hour's conversation, Beauty discovered that the terrible tone of his voice was attributable only to the nature of the organ; and that the Beast was more inclined to stupidity than to ferocity. At length he asked her bluntly if she would marry him. At this unexpected demand, her fears were renewed, and uttering a terrible shriek, she could not help exclaiming, "Heavens, I am lost!"

"Not at all," replied the Beast quietly, "but without frightening yourself, reply properly. Say precisely 'yes' or 'no'."

Beauty replied, trembling, "No, Beast."

"Well, as you object, I will leave you," replied the docile Beast. "Good evening, Beauty."

"Good evening, Beast," said the frightened girl, with much satisfaction.

Extremely relieved by finding that she had no violence to fear, she lay quietly down and went to sleep. Immediately her dear unknown returned to her mind. He appeared to say to her, tenderly, "How overjoyed I am to see you once more, dear Beauty, but what pain has your severity caused me? I know that I must expect to be unhappy for a long time."

Her ideas again changed, the young man appeared to offer her a crown and sleep presented him to her in a hundred different manners. Sometimes he seemed to be at her feet, sometimes abandoning himself to the most excessive delight, at others shedding a torrent of tears, which touched the depths of her soul. This mixture of joy and sadness lasted all the night.

On waking, having her imagination full of this dear object, she sought for his portrait, to compare it once more with her recollections, and to see if she were not deceived. She ran to the picture gallery, where she recognised him still more perfectly. How long she was admiring him! But feeling ashamed of her weakness, she contented herself at length by looking at the miniature on her arm.

CHAPTER V
EXPLORING THE PALACE OF THE BEAST

To put an end to her tender reflections, Beauty descended into the palace garden, the fine weather seeming to invite her to a stroll. Her eyes were enchanted; they had never seen anything in nature so beautiful. The groves were ornamented with admirable statues and numberless fountains, which cooled the air, and shot up to such a height that the eye could scarcely follow them.

What surprised her most was that she recognised the places wherein she had dreamt she had seen the Unknown. Especially at the sight of the Grand Canal, bordered with orange and myrtle trees, she could not but think of her vision, which appeared no longer a fiction. She thought to explain the mystery by imagining that the Beast kept someone shut up in his palace. She resolved to be enlightened on the subject that same evening, and to question the Beast, from whom she expected a visit at the usual hour. She walked for the rest of the day, as long as her strength permitted, without being able to see all.

The apartments, which she had not been able to inspect the evening before, were no less worthy of her admiration than the others. Besides the instruments and curiosities with which she was surrounded, she found in another cabinet plenty to occupy her. It was tilled with purses, and shuttles for knotting, scissors for cutting out, and fitted up for all sorts of ladies' work; in fact, everything was to be found there.

In this gallery, care had been taken to place a cage filled with rare birds, all of which, on the arrival of Beauty, formed an admirable concert. They came also and perched on her shoulders, and these loving little creatures vied with each other as to which should nestle closest to her. "Amiable prisoners," she said, "I think you charming, and I am vexed that you should be so far from my apartment, I should often like the pleasure of hearing you sing."

What was her surprise, when as she said these words, she opened a door and found herself in her own chamber, which she believed was very distant from this gallery, having only arrived in it after turning and threading a labyrinth of apartments which composed this pavilion. A panel which had concealed from her the neighbourhood of the birds, opened into the gallery, and was very convenient, as it completely shut out the noise of them when quiet was desirable.

Beauty, continuing her route, perceived another feathered group; these were parrots of all kinds and of all colours. All at her approach began to chatter. One said, "Good day" to her; the other asked her for some breakfast; one more gallant begged a kiss; several sang opera airs, others declaimed verses composed by the best authors; and all exerted themselves to entertain her. They were as gentle and as affectionate as the inhabitants of the aviary.

Their presence was a real pleasure to her. She was delighted to find something she could talk with, for silence was not agreeable to her. She put several questions to some of them, who answered her like very intelligent creatures. She selected one from amongst them as the most amusing. The others, jealous of this preference, complained sadly. She consoled them by some caresses, and the permission to pay her a visit whenever they pleased.

Not far from this spot, she saw a numerous troop of monkeys of all sizes, great and small, Sapajous, some with human faces, others with beards, blue, green, black, and crimson. They advanced to meet her at the door of their apartment, which she had by chance arrived at. They made her low bows, accompanied by countless capers, and testified, by action, how highly sensible they were of the honour she had done them. To celebrate her visit, they danced upon the tightrope, and bounded about with a skill and agility beyond example.

Beauty was much pleased with the monkeys, but she was disappointed at not finding anything which could enlighten her respecting the handsome Unknown. Losing all hope of doing so, and looking upon her dream as altogether an illusion, she did her best to drive the recollection of it from her mind; but her efforts were vain.

She praised the monkeys, and, caressing them, said she should like some of them to follow her and keep her company. Instantly two tall young apes, in court dresses - who appeared to have been only waiting for her orders - advanced and placed themselves with great gravity beside her. Two sprightly little monkeys took up her train as her pages. A facetious baboon, dressed as a Spanish gentleman of the chamber, presented his paw to her, very neatly gloved, and accompanied by this singular cortege, Beauty proceeded to the supper table.

During her meal the smaller birds whistled, in perfect tune, an accompaniment to the voices of the parrots, who sang the finest and most fashionable airs. During the concert, the monkeys - who had taken upon themselves the right of attending upon Beauty - having in an instant settled their several ranks and duties, commenced their service, and waited on her in full state, with all the attention and respect that officers of a royal household are accustomed to pay to Queens.

On rising from table, another troop proceeded to entertain her with a novel spectacle. They were a sort of company of actors, who played a tragedy in the most extraordinary fashion. These *Signor* Monkeys and *Signora* Apes, in stage dresses covered with embroidery, pearls, and diamonds, executed all the actions suitable to the words of their parts, which were spoken with great distinctness and proper emphasis by the parrots; so cleverly, indeed, that it was necessary to be assured that these birds were concealed in the wig of one actor or under the mantle of another, not to believe that these new-fashioned tragedians were speaking themselves.

The drama appeared to have been written expressly for the actors, and Beauty was enchanted. At the end of the tragedy, one of the performers advanced and paid Beauty a very well-turned compliment, and thanked her for the indulgence with which she had listened to them. All then departed, except the monkeys of her household, and those selected to keep her company.

After supper, the Beast paid her his usual visit, and after the same questions and the same answers, the conversation ended with a "Good night, Beauty". The Lady-Apes of the bedchamber undressed their mistress, put her to bed, and took care to open the window of the aviary, which the birds, by a warbling much softer than their songs by day, might induce slumber, and afford her the pleasure of again beholding her lover.

Several days passed without her experiencing any feeling of dullness. Every moment brought with it fresh pleasures. The monkeys, in three or four lessons, succeeded each one in teaching a parrot, who, acting as an interpreter, replied to Beauty's questions with as much promptitude and accuracy as the monkeys themselves had done by gestures.

In fine, Beauty found nothing to complain of but the obligation of enduring every evening the presence of the Beast; but his visits were short, and it was undoubtedly to him that she was indebted for the enjoyment of all imaginable amusements.

The gentleness of the Beast occasionally inspired Beauty with the idea of asking some explanation respecting the person she saw in her dreams; but sufficiently aware that he was in love with her, and fearing by such questioning to awaken his jealousy, she had the prudence to remain silent and did not venture to satisfy her curiosity.

By degrees she had visited every apartment in this enchanted palace: but one willingly returns to the inspection of things which are rare, singular, and costly. Beauty turned her steps towards a great saloon, which she had only seen once before. This room had four windows in it on each side. Two only were open, and admitted a glimmering light. Beauty wished for more light, but in lieu of obtaining any by opening another window, she found it only looked into some enclosed space, which, although large, was obscure, and her eyes could distinguish nothing but a distant gleam, which appeared to reach them through the medium of a very thick crape.

Whilst pondering for what purpose this place could have been designed, she was suddenly dazzled by a brilliant illumination. The curtain rose and discovered to Beauty a theatre, exceedingly well lighted. On the benches and in the boxes she beheld all that was most handsome and well made of either sex. A sweet symphony, which instantly commenced, terminated only to permit other actors than monkey and parrot performers to represent a very fine tragedy, which was followed by a little piece, quite equal in its own style to that which had preceded it.

Beauty was fond of plays. It was the only pleasure she had regretted when she left the city. Desiring to ascertain what sort of material the hangings of the box next to her were made of, she found herself prevented doing so by a glass which separated them, and thereby discovered that what she had seen were not the actual objects, but a reflection of them by means of this crystal mirror, which thus conveyed to her sight all that was passing on the stage of the finest city in the world, it is a master-stroke in optics to be able to reflect from such a distance. She remained in her box some time after the play was over, in order to see the fine company go out.

The darkness that gradually ensued compelled her to think of other matters. Satisfied with this discovery, of which she promised to avail herself often, she descended into the gardens. Prodigies were becoming familiar to her. She rejoiced to find they were all performed for her advantage and amusement.

After supper, the Beast came, as usual, to ask her what she had been doing during the day. Beauty gave him an exact account of all her amusements, and told him she had been to the play. "Do you like it?" inquired the dull creature. "Wish for whatever you please, you shall have it. You are very handsome."

Beauty smiled to herself at the coarse manner in which he paid her compliments; but what she did not smile at was the usual question, and the words "Will you marry me?" put an end to her good humour. She had only to answer "No;" but, nevertheless, his docility during this last interview did not reassure her. Beauty was alarmed at it. *"What is to be the end of all this?" she said to herself. "The question he puts to me every time, 'Will I marry him', proves that he persists in loving me: his bounty to me confirms it. But though he does not insist on my compliance nor show any signs of resentment at my refusal, who will be answerable to me that he do not eventually lose his patience, and that my death will not be the consequence?"*

These reflections rendered her so thoughtful that it was almost daylight before she went to bed. The Unknown, who but awaited that moment to appear, reproached her tenderly for her delay He found her melancholy, lost in thought, and inquired what could have displeased her in such a place. She answered that nothing displeased her, except the Beast whom she saw every evening. She should have become accustomed to him but he was in love with her, and this love made her apprehensive of some violence.

"By the foolish compliments he pays me," said Beauty to her lover, "I find he desires to marry me. Would you advise me to consent? Alas! Were he as charming as he is frightful, you have rendered my heart inaccessible to him and to all others; and I do not blush to own that I can love no one but you."

So sweet a confession could but flatter the Unknown, yet he replied to her only by saying, "Love him who loves you. Do not be misled by appearances, and release me from prison."

These words, continually repeated without any explanation, caused Beauty infinite distress. "What would you that I should do?" said she to him. "I would restore you to liberty at any price; but my desire is vain while you abstain from furnishing me with the means to put it in practice."

The Unknown made her some answer, but of so confused a nature that she could not comprehend it. A thousand extravagant fancies passed before her eyes. She saw the Beast on a throne all blazing with jewels; he called to her and invited her to sit beside him. A moment afterwards, the Unknown compelled him precipitately to descend, and seated himself in his place. The Beast regaining the advantage, the Unknown disappeared in his turn. He spoke to her from behind a black veil, which changed his voice, and rendered it horrible.

All her sleep passed in this manner, and yet, notwithstanding the agitation it caused her, she felt it was too soon over, as her awakening deprived her of the sight of the object of her affections.

After she had finished dressing, various sorts of work, books, and animals occupied her attention until the hour when the play began. She arrived just in time, but she was not at the same theatre. It was the opera and the performance commenced as soon as she was seated.

The spectacle was magnificent, and the spectators were not less so. The mirrors represented to her distinctly the minutest details of the dresses even of the people in the pit. Delighted to behold human forms and faces, many of which she recognised as those of persons she knew, it would have been a still greater pleasure to her could she have spoken to them, so that they could have heard her.

More gratified with this day's entertainment than with that of the preceding, the rest of it passed in the same way that each had done since she had been in that palace. The Beast came in the evening, and after his visit she retired, as usual.

The night resembled former nights, that is, it was passed in agreeable dreams. When she awoke, she found the same number of domestics to wait upon her; but after dinner, her occupations were different. The day before, on opening another of the windows, she had found herself at the opera.

To diversify her amusements, she now opened a third window, which displayed to her all the pleasures of the Fair of St. Germain, much more brilliant then than it is at the present day. But as the hour had not quite arrived when the best company resorted to it, she had leisure to observe and examine everything.

She saw the rarest curiosities, the most extraordinary productions of nature and works of art. The minutest trifles were visible to her. The puppet-show was not unworthy of her attention, whilst waiting for more refined entertainments. The comic opera was in its splendour. Beauty was very much delighted.

At the termination of the performances, she saw all the well-dressed people visiting the tradesmen's shops. She recognised amongst the crowd several professional gamesters, who flocked to this place as their workshop. She observed persons who, having lost their money by the cleverness of those they played with, went out with less joyous countenances than they exhibited as they entered. The prudent gamblers, who did not stake their whole fortunes on the hazard of a card, and who played to profit by their skill, could not conceal from Beauty their sleight of hand. She longed to warn the victims of the tricks they were plundered by; but at a distance from them of more than a thousand leagues, it was not in her power to do so. She heard and saw everything distinctly, without its being possible for her to make herself heard or seen by others. The reflections and echoes, which conveyed to her all these sights and sounds, had no returning power. Placed above the air and wind, everything came to her like a thought. The consideration of this fact deterred her from making vain attempts.

It was past midnight before she thought it was time to retire. The need of some refreshment might have hinted to her the lateness of the hour; but she had found in her box liqueurs and baskets filled with everything requisite for a collation. Her supper was light and of short duration; she was in a hurry to go to bed. The Beast observed her impatience, and came merely to say goodnight, that she might have more time to sleep and the Unknown liberty to reappear.

The following days resembled each other. She found in her windows an inexhaustible source of fresh entertainments. The first of the other three afforded her the pleasure of witnessing Italian comedy, the second a sight of the Tuileries, the resort of all the most distinguished and handsome of both sexes.

The last window was very far from being the least agreeable. It enabled her to see everything of consequence that was going on in the world. The scene was amusing and interesting in all sorts of ways. Sometimes it was the reception of a grand embassy, at others the marriage of some illustrious personages, and occasionally some exciting revolutions. She was at this window during the last revolt of the Janizaries, and witnessed the whole of it to the very end.

At all times she was certain to find something here to entertain her. The weariness she had felt at first in listening to the Beast had entirely departed. Her eyes had become accustomed to his ugliness. She was prepared for his foolish questions, and if their conversations had lasted longer, perchance she would have not been displeased; but four or five sentences, always the same, uttered in a coarse manner, and productive only of a "Yes" or "No", were not much to her taste.

As the slightest desires of Beauty appeared to be anticipated, she bestowed more care upon her toilet, although certain that no one could see her. But she owed this attention to herself, and it was a pleasure to her to dress herself in the habits of all the various nations on the face of the earth.

She could do this the more easily, as her wardrobe furnished her with everything she chose, and presented her every day with some novelty. Contemplating her mirror in these various dresses, it revealed to her that she was to be admired in all lands; and her attendant animals, each according to their talent, repeated to her unceasingly the same fact - the monkeys by their actions, the parrots by their language, and the other birds by their songs.

So delightful a life ought to have perfectly contented her, but we weary of everything. The greatest happiness fades when it is continual, derived always from the same source, and we find ourselves exempted from fear and from hope. Beauty had experienced this. The remembrance of her family arose to trouble her in the midst of her prosperity. Her happiness could not be perfect as long as she was denied the pleasure of informing her relations of it.

As she had become more familiar with the Beast, either from the habit of seeing him or from the gentleness which she had discovered in his nature, she thought she might venture to ask him a question. She did not take this liberty, however, until she had obtained from him a promise that he would not be angry. The question she put to him was, "Were they the only two persons in that palace?"

"Yes, I protest to you," replied the Beast, in a rather excited tone; "and I assure you that you and I, the monkeys, and the other animals, are the only breathing creatures in this place." The Beast said no more, and departed more abruptly than usual.

Beauty had asked this question only with a view of ascertaining whether her lover was not confined in the palace. She would have wished to see and speak with him. It was a happiness she would have purchased at the price of her own liberty and of all the pleasures by which she was surrounded. That charming youth existing only in her imagination, she now looked upon this palace as a prison which would be one day her tomb.

These melancholy ideas crowded also upon her mind at night. She dreamed she was on the banks of a great canal; she was weeping, when her dear Unknown, alarmed at her sad state, said to her, pressing her hand tenderly between his own, "What is the matter, my beloved Beauty? Who can have offended you, and what can possibly have disturbed your tranquillity? By the love I bear you, I conjure you to explain the cause of your distress. Nothing shall be refused to you. You are sole sovereign here, everything is at your command. Whence arises the sorrow that overpowers you? Is it the sight of the Beast that afflicts you? You must be relieved from it!"

At these words Beauty imagined she saw the Unknown draw a dagger, and prepare to plunge it in the throat of the Beast, who made no attempt to defend himself, but, on the contrary, offered his neck to the blow with a submission and a calmness which caused the beautiful dreamer to fear the

Unknown would accomplish his purpose before she could endeavour to prevent him, notwithstanding she had instantly risen to protect the Beast. The instant she saw her efforts likely to be anticipated, she exclaimed, with all her might, "Hold, barbarian! Harm not my benefactor, or else kill me!"

The Unknown, who continued striking at the Beast, notwithstanding the shrieks of Beauty, said to her, angrily, "You love me, then, no longer, since you take the part of this Beast, who is an obstacle to my happiness!"

"You are ungrateful," she replied, still struggling with him; "I love you more than my life, and I would lose it sooner than cease to love you. You are the world to me, and I would not do you the injustice to compare you with any other treasure it possesses. I would, without a sigh, abandon all it could offer me, to follow you into the wildest desert. But this tender affection does not stifle my gratitude. I owe everything to the Beast. He anticipates all my wishes: it is to him I am indebted for the joy of knowing you, and I would die sooner than endure seeing you do him the slightest injury."

After several similar struggles the objects vanished, and Beauty fancied she saw the lady who had appeared to her some nights before, and who said to her, "Courage, Beauty; be a model of female generosity; show yourself to be as wise as you are charming; do not hesitate to sacrifice your inclination to your duty. You are taking the true path to happiness. You will be blessed, provided you are not misled by deceitful appearances."

When Beauty awoke she pondered on this mysterious vision, but it still remained an enigma to her. Her desire to see her father superseded, during the day, the anxiety caused by these dreams of the Beast and the Unknown. Thus, neither tranquil at night nor contented by day, although surrounded by the greatest luxuries, the only distraction she could find was in the theatre.

She went to the Italians, but after the first scene she quitted that performance for the Opera, which she left almost as quickly. Her melancholy followed her everywhere. She frequently opened each of the six windows as many times without finding one minute's respite from her cares. Days and nights of equal and unceasing agitation began seriously to affect her appearance and her health.

CHAPTER VI
BEAUTY'S VISIT TO HER FAMILY

Beauty took great pains to conceal from the Beast the sorrow which preyed upon her; and the Beast, who had frequently surprised her with the tears in her eyes, upon hearing her say that she was only suffering from a headache, pressed his inquiries no further. One evening, however, her sobs having betrayed her, and feeling it impossible longer to dissimulate, she acknowledged to the Beast - who begged to know what had caused her afflictions - that she was yearning to see her family.

At this declaration the Beast sank down without power to sustain himself, and heaving a deep sigh, or rather uttering a howl that might have frightened any one to death, he replied, "How, Beauty! Would you, then, abandon an unfortunate Beast? Could I have imagined you possessed so little gratitude? What have I left undone to make you happy? Should not the attentions I have paid you preserve me from your hatred? Unjust as you are, you prefer the house of your father and the jealousy of your sisters to my palace and my affections. You would rather tend the flocks with them than enjoy with me all the pleasures of existence. It is not love for your family, but antipathy to me, that makes you anxious to depart."

"No, Beast," replied Beauty, timidly and soothingly; "I do

not hate you, and should regret to lose the hope of seeing you again; but I cannot overcome the desire I feel to embrace my relations. Permit me to go away for two months, and I promise you that I will return with pleasure to pass the rest of my days with you, and never ask you another favour."

While she spoke the Beast stretched on the ground, his head thrown back, only evinced that he still breathed by his sorrowful sighs. He answered her in these words: "I can refuse you nothing; but it will perhaps cost me my life. No matter. In the cabinet nearest to your apartment you will find four chests. Fill them with anything you like for yourself or for your family. If you break your word you will repent it, and regret the death of your poor Beast when it will be too late. Return at the end of two months, and you will still see me alive.

"For your journey back to me you will need no equipage. Merely take leave of your family the previous night before you retire to rest, and when you are in bed turn your ring, the stone inside your hand, and say, with a firm voice, 'I desire to return to my palace, and behold my Beast again.' Goodnight; fear nothing; sleep in peace. You will see your father early tomorrow morning. *Adieu, Beauty.*"

As soon as she was alone she hastened to fill the chests with all the treasures and beautiful things imaginable. They only appeared to be full when she was tired of putting things into them. After these preparations, she went to bed. The thoughts of seeing her family so soon kept her awake great part of the night, and sleep only stole upon her towards the hour when she should have been stirring. She saw in her dreams her amiable Unknown, but not as formerly.

Stretched upon a bed of turf, he appeared a prey to the keenest sorrow. Beauty, touched at seeing him in such a state, flattered herself she could alleviate his profound affliction by requesting to know the cause of it; but her lover, casting on her a look full of despair, said, "Can you ask me such a question, inhuman girl? Are you not aware that your departure dooms me to death?"

"Abandon not yourself to sorrow, dear Unknown," she replied, "my absence will be brief. I wish but to undeceive my family respecting the cruel fate they imagine has befallen me. I return immediately afterwards to this palace. I shall leave you no more. Ah! Could I abandon a residence in which I so delight! Besides, I have pledged my word to the Beast that I will return. I cannot fail to keep it; and why must this journey separate us? Be my escort. I will defer my departure another day in order to obtain the Beast's permission. I am sure he will not refuse me. Agree to my proposal, and we shall not part. We will return together; my family will be delighted to see you, and I will answer for their showing you all the attention you deserve."

"I cannot accede to your wishes," replied the Unknown, "unless you determine never to return here. It is the only means of enabling me to quit this spot. How will you decide? The inhabitants of this palace have no power to compel you to return. Nothing can happen to you beyond the knowledge that you have grieved the Beast."

"You do not consider," rejoined Beauty, quickly, "that he assured me he should die if I broke my word to him."

"What matters it to you?" retorted her lover. "Is it to be counted a misfortune that your happiness should cost only the life of a Beast? Of what use is he to the world? Will anyone be a loser by the destruction of a being who appears upon earth only to be the horror of all nature?"

"Ha!" exclaimed Beauty, almost angrily, "know that I

would lay down my life to save his, and that this Beast, who is only one in form, has a heart so humane, that he should not be persecuted for a deformity which he refrains from rendering more hideous by his actions. I will not repay his kindness with such black ingratitude."

The Unknown, interrupting her, inquired what she would do if the Beast endeavoured to kill him; and, if it were decreed that one of them must slay the other, to which would she afford assistance? "I love you only," she replied; "but extreme as is my affection for you, it cannot weaken my gratitude to the Beast, and if I found myself placed in so fatal a position, I would escape the misery which the result of such a combat would inflict on me, by dying by my own hand. But why indulge in such dreadful suppositions? However fanciful, the idea freezes my blood; let us change the conversation."

She set him the example, by saying all that an affectionate girl could say, most flattering to her lover. She was not restrained by the rigid customs of society, and slumber left her free to act naturally. She acknowledged to him her love with a frankness which she would have shrunk from when in full possession of her reason. Her sleep was of long duration, and when she awoke she feared the Beast had failed in his promise to her. She was in this uncertainty when she heard the sound of a human voice which she recognised.

Drawing her curtains precipitately, what was her surprise when she found herself in a strange apartment, the furniture of which was not near as superb as that in the Palace of the Beast. This prodigy induced her to rise hastily, and open the door of her chamber. The next room was equally strange to her; but what astonished her still more, was to find in it the four chests she had filled the previous evening.

The transport of herself and her treasures was a proof of the power and bounty of the Beast - but where was she? She could not imagine; when at length she heard the voice of her father, and rushing out, she flung her arms round his neck. Her appearance astounded her brothers and sisters. They stared at her as at one come from the other world. All her family embraced her with the greatest demonstrations of delight; but her sisters, in their hearts, were vexed at beholding her. Their jealousy was not extinguished.

After many caresses on both sides, the good man desired to speak with her privately, to learn from her own lips all the circumstances of so extraordinary a journey, and to inform her of the state of his own fortune, of which he had set apart a large share for herself. He told her that on the evening of the same day that he had left the Palace of the Beast, he had reached his own house without the least fatigue. That on the road he had cogitated how he could best manage to conceal his trunks from the sight of his children, and wished that they could be carried without their knowledge into a little cabinet adjoining his bedchamber, of which he alone had the key. That he had looked upon this as impossible; but that, on dismounting at his door, he found the horse on which his trunks had been placed had run away, and therefore saw himself suddenly spared the trouble of hiding his treasures.

"I assure you," said the old man to his daughter, "that the loss of these riches did not distress me. I had not possessed them long enough to regret them greatly; but the adventure appeared to me a gloomy prognostic of my fate. I did not hesitate to believe that the perfidious Beast would act in the same manner by you. I feared that the favours he conferred upon you would not be more durable. This idea caused me great anxiety.

"To conceal it, I feigned to be in need of rest, it was only to abandon myself without restraint to my grief. I looked upon your destruction as certain, but my sorrow was soon dissipated. The sight of the trunks I thought I had lost renewed my hopes of your happiness. I found them placed in my little cabinet, precisely where I had wished them to be. The keys of them, which I had forgotten and left behind me on the table in the saloon wherein we had passed the night, were in the locks.

"This circumstance, which afforded me a new proof of the kindness of the Beast, and his constant attention, overwhelmed me with joy. It was then that, no longer doubting the advantageous result of your adventure, I reproached myself for entertaining such unjust suspicions of the honour of that generous Beast, and craved his pardon a hundred times for the abuse which, in my distress, I had mentally lavished upon him.

"Without informing my children of the extent of my wealth, I contented myself with distributing amongst them the presents you had sent them, and showing them some jewels of moderate value. I afterwards pretended to have sold them, and have employed the money in various ways for the improvement of our income. I have bought this house; I have slaves, who relieve us from the labours to which necessity had subjected us. My children lead an easy life, which is all I care for. Ostentation and luxury drew upon me, in other days, the hatred of the envious; I should incur it again did I live in the style of a very wealthy man.

"Many offers have been made to your sisters, Beauty; I am about to marry them off immediately, and your fortunate arrival decides me. Having given to them such portions of the wealth you have brought to me, as you shall think fit, and relieved of all care for their establishment, we will live, my daughter, with your brothers, whom your presents were not able to console for your loss; or, if you prefer it, we two will live together independently of them."

Beauty, affected by the kindness of her father, and the assurance he gave her of the love of her brothers, thanked him tenderly for all his offers, and thought it would be wrong to conceal from him the fact that she had not come to stay with him. The good man, distressed to learn that he should not have the support of his child in his declining years, did not, however, attempt to dissuade her from the fulfilment of a duty which he acknowledged indispensable.

Beauty, in her turn, related to him all that had happened to her since they parted. She described to him the pleasant life she led. The good man, enraptured at the charming account of his daughter's adventures, heaped blessings on the head of the Beast. His delight was much greater still when Beauty, opening the chests, displayed to him the immense treasures they contained, and satisfied him that he was at liberty to dispose of those which he had brought himself, in favour of his daughters, as he would possess, in these last proofs of the Beast's generosity, ample means to live merrily with his sons.

Discovering in this Beast too noble a mind to be lodged in so hideous a body, he deemed it his duty to advise his daughter to marry him, notwithstanding his ugliness. He employed even the strongest arguments to induce her to take that step.

"You should not take counsel from your eyes alone," he said to her. "You have been unceasingly exhorted to let yourself be guided by gratitude. By following her inspirations you are assured you will be happy. It is true these warnings are only given you in dreams; but these dreams are too significant and too frequent to be attributed to chance. They promise you great advantages, enough to conquer your repugnance.

"Therefore, the next time that the Beast asks you if you will marry him, I advise you not to refuse him. You have admitted to me that he loves you tenderly: take the proper means to make your union with him indissoluble. It is much better to have an amiable husband than one whose only recommendation is a handsome person. How many girls are compelled to marry rich brutes, much more brutish than the Beast, who is only one in form, and not in his feelings or his actions?"

Beauty admitted the reason of all these arguments; but to resolve to marry a Beast so horrible in person and who seemed as stupid as he was gigantic, appeared to her an impossibility. "How can I determine," she replied to her father, "to take a husband with whom I can have no sympathy, and whose hideousness is not compensated for by the charms of his conversation? No other object to distract my attention and relieve that wearisome companionship; not to have the pleasure of being sometimes absent from him; to hear nothing beyond five or six questions respecting my health or my appetite, followed by a 'Goodnight, Beauty', a chorus which my parrots know by heart, and repeat a hundred times a day.

"It is not in my power to endure such a union, and I would rather perish at once than be dying every day of fright, sorrow, disgust, and weariness. There is nothing to plead in his favour, except the consideration he evinces in paying me very short visits and presenting himself before me but once in four-and-twenty hours. Is that enough to inspire one with affection?"

The father admitted that his daughter had reason on her side, but observing so much civility in the Beast, he could not believe him to be as stupid as she represented him. The order, the abundance, the good taste that was discernible through his palace, were not, according to his thinking, the work of a fool.

In fact, he found him worthy of the consideration of his daughter, and Beauty might have felt more inclined to listen to the Beast, had not her nocturnal lover's appearance thrown an obstacle in the way. The comparison she drew between these two admirers could not be favourable to the Beast. The old man himself was fully aware of the great distinction which must be made between them. Notwithstanding, he tried by all manner of means to overcome her repugnance. He recalled to her the advice of the lady who had warned her not to be prejudiced by appearances, and whose language seemed to imply that this youth would only make her miserable.

It is easier to reason with love than to conquer it. Beauty had not the power to yield to the reiterated requests of her father. He left her without having been able to persuade her. Night, already far advanced, invited her to repose, and the daughter, although delighted to see her father once more, was not sorry that he left her at liberty to retire to rest. She was glad to be alone.

Her heavy eyelids inspired her with the hope that in slumber she would soon again behold her beloved Unknown. She was eager to enjoy this innocent pleasure. A quickened pulsation evinced the joy with which her gentle heart would greet that pleasant vision; but her excited imagination, while representing to her the scenes in which she had usually held sweet converse with that dear Unknown, had not sufficient power to conjure up his form to her as she so ardently desired.

She awoke several times, but on falling asleep again no Cupids fluttered round her couch. In a word, instead of a night full of sweet thoughts and innocent pleasures, which she had counted on passing in the arms of sleep, it was to her one of interminable length and endless anxiety. She had never known any like it in the Palace of the Beast, and the day, which she at last saw break with a mingled feeling of satisfaction and impatience, came opportunely to relieve her from this weariness.

Her father, enriched by the liberality of the Beast, had quitted his country house, and in order to facilitate the establishment of his daughters, resided in a very large city, where his new fortune obtained for him new friends, or rather new acquaintances.

Amidst the circle who visited him the tidings soon spread that his youngest daughter had returned. Everybody evinced an equal impatience to see her and was each as much charmed with her intellect as with her beauty. The peaceful days she had passed in her desert palace, the innocent pleasures which a gentle slumber had invariably procured her, the thousand amusements which succeeded, so that dullness could never take possession of her spirit, in brief, all the attentions of the Beast had combined to render her still more beautiful and more charming than she was when her father first parted from her.

She was the admiration of all who saw her. The suitors to her sisters, without condescending to excuse their infidelity by the slightest pretext, fell in love with her, and attracted by the power of her charms, deserted, without a blush, their former mistresses. Insensible to the marked attentions of a crowd of adorers, she neglected nothing that could discourage them and induce them to return to the previous objects of their affection; but, notwithstanding all her care, she could not escape the jealousy of her sisters.

The inconstant lovers, far from concealing their new

passion, invented every day some fresh entertainment, with the view of paying their court to her. They entreated her even to bestow the prize in the games which took place in her honour; but Beauty, who could not be blind to the mortification she was causing her sisters, and yet was unwilling to refuse utterly the favour they implored so ardently, and in so flattering a manner, found means to satisfy them all, by declaring that she would, alternately with her sisters, present the prize to the victor.

What she selected was a flower or some equally simple guerdon. She left to her elder sisters the honour of giving, in their turn, jewels, crowns of diamonds, costly weapons, or superb bracelets, presents which her liberal hand supplied them with, but for which she would not take the slightest credit. The treasures lavished on her by the Beast left her in want of nothing. She divided between her sisters everything she had brought that was most rare and elegant. Bestowing nothing but trifles herself, and leaving them the pleasure of giving largely, she counted on securing for them the love as well as the gratitude of the youthful combatants. But these lovers sought only to gain her heart, and the simplest gift from her hand was more precious to them than all the treasures that were prodigally heaped upon them by the others.

The amusements she partook of amongst her family, though vastly inferior to those she enjoyed in the Palace of the Beast, entertained her sufficiently to prevent the time hanging heavily on her hands. At the same time, neither the gratification of seeing her father, whom she tenderly loved, nor the pleasure of being with her brothers, who in a hundred ways studied to prove to her the extent of their affection, nor the delight of conversing with her sisters, of whom she was very fond - though they were not so of her - could prevent her regretting her agreeable dreams.

Her Unknown (greatly to her sorrow) came not, when she slumbered under her father's roof, to address her in the most tender language; and the court paid to her by those who had been the admirers of her sisters, did not compensate for the loss of that pleasing illusion. Had she even been of a nature to feel flattered by such conquests, she would still have distinguished an immense difference between their attentions, or those of the Beast, and the devotion of her charming Unknown.

Their assiduities were received by her with the greatest indifference; but Beauty perceiving that, notwithstanding her coolness, they were obstinately bent on rivalling each other in the task of proving to her the intensity of their passion, thought it her duty to make them clearly understand they were losing their time.

The first she endeavoured to undeceive was one who had courted her eldest sister. She told him that she had only returned for the purpose of being present at the marriage of her sisters, particularly that of her eldest sister, and that she was about to press her father to settle it immediately. Beauty found that she had to deal with a man who saw no longer any charms in her sister. He sighed alone for her, and coldness, disdain, the threat to depart before the expiration of the two months nothing, in short, could discourage him. Much vexed at having failed in her object, she held a similar conversation with the others, whom she had the mortification to find equally infatuated.

To complete her distress, her unjust sisters, who looked upon her as a rival, conceived a hatred for her which they could not dissemble; and whilst Beauty was deploring the too great power of her charms, she had the misery of learning that her new adorers, believing each to be the cause of the other's rejection, were bent, in the maddest way, on fighting it out amongst themselves. All these annoyances induced her to determine upon returning sooner than she had contemplated.

Her father and brothers did all they could to detain her; but the slave of her word, and firm in resolution, neither the tears of the one nor the prayers of the others could prevail upon her. All that they could extort from her was that she would defer her departure as long as she could. The two months had nearly expired, and every morning she determined to bid *Adieu* to her family, without having the heart when night arrived to say farewell. In the combat between her affection and her gratitude, she could not lean to the one without doing injustice to the other.

In the midst of her embarrassment, it needed nothing less than a dream to decide her. She fancied she was at the Palace of the Beast, and walking in a retired avenue, terminated by a thicket full of brambles, concealing the entrance to a cavern, out of which issued horrible groans.

She recognised the voice of the Beast, and ran to his assistance. The Beast, who, in her dream, appeared stretched upon the ground and dying, reproached her with being the cause of his death, and having repaid his affection with the blackest ingratitude. She then saw the lady who had before appeared to her in her sleep, and who said to her in a severe tone, that it would be her destruction if she hesitated any longer to fulfil her engagements; that she had given her word to the Beast that she would return in two months; that the time had expired; that the delay of another day would be fatal to the Beast; that the trouble she was creating in her father's house and the hatred of her sisters ought to increase her desire to return to the Palace of the Beast, where everything combined to delight her.

Beauty, terrified by this dream, and fearing to be the cause of the death of the Beast, awoke with a start, and went immediately to inform her family that she could no longer delay her departure. This intelligence produced various effects. Her father's tears spoke for him; her brothers protested that they would not allow her to leave them; and her lovers, in despair, swore they would not suffer the house to be robbed of its brightest ornament.

Her sisters alone, far from appearing distressed at her departure, were loud in praise of her sense of honour; and affecting to possess the same virtue themselves, had the audacity to assure her that if they had pledged their words to the Beast as she had done, they should not have suffered his ugliness to have interfered with their feelings of duty, and that they should have long ere that time been on their road back to the marvellous palace. It was thus they endeavoured to disguise the cruel jealousy that rankled in their hearts.

Beauty, however, charmed by their apparent generosity, thought only of convincing her brothers and her lovers of the obligation she was under to leave them; but her brothers loved her too much to consent to her going and her lovers were too infatuated to listen to reason. All of them being ignorant of the mode in which Beauty had arrived at her father's house, and never doubting but that the horse which first conveyed her to the Palace of the Beast would be sent to take her back again, resolved amongst themselves to prevent it.

Her sisters, who only concealed their delight by the affectation of a sentiment of horror, as they perceived the hour approach for Beauty's departure, were frightened to death lest anything should occur to delay her; but Beauty, firm in her resolution, knowing whither duty called her, and having no more time to lose, if she would prolong the existence of the Beast, her benefactor, at nightfall took leave of her family, and of all those who were interested in her destiny.

She assured them that whatever steps they took to prevent her departure, she should, nevertheless, be in the Palace of the Beast the next morning before they were stirring; that all their schemes would be fruitless; and that she had determined to return to the Enchanted Palace. She did not forget, on going to bed, to turn her ring.

CHAPTER VII
THE FUTURE OF THE BEAST

Beauty slept very soundly, and did not awake until the clock in her chamber, striking noon, chimed her name to music. By that sound she knew that her wishes were accomplished. As soon as she evinced a disposition to rise, her couch was surrounded by all the animals that had been so eager to serve her, and who unanimously testified their gratification at her return, and expressed the sorrow they had felt at her long absence.

The day seemed to her longer than any she had previously passed in that Palace, not so much from regret for those she had quitted as from her impatience again to behold the Beast, and to say everything she could to him in the way of excuse for her conduct. She was also animated by another desire - that of again holding in slumber one of those sweet conversations with her dear Unknown, a pleasure she had been deprived of during the two months she had passed with her family, and which she could not enjoy anywhere but in that Palace.

The Beast and the Unknown were, in short, alternately the subjects of her reflections. One moment, she reproached herself for not returning the affection of a lover who, under the form of a Beast, displayed so noble a mind; the next she

67

deplored having set her heart upon a visionary object that had no existence except in her dreams. She began to doubt whether she ought to prefer the imaginary devotion of a phantom to the real affection of the Beast. The very dream in which the Unknown appeared to her was invariably accompanied by warnings not to trust to sight. She feared it was but an idle illusion, born of the vapours of the brain, and destroyed by light of day.

Thus undecided, loving the Unknown, yet not wishing to displease the Beast, and seeking repose from her thoughts in some entertainment, she went to the French Comedy, which she found exceedingly poor. Shutting the window abruptly, she hoped to be better pleased at the Opera. She thought the music miserable. The Italians were equally unable to amuse her. Their comedy appeared to her to want smartness, wit and action. Weariness and distaste accompanied her everywhere, and prevented her taking pleasure in anything.

The gardens had no attractions for her. Her Court endeavoured to entertain her, but the monkeys lost their labour in frisking, and the parrots and other birds in chattering and singing. She was impatient for the visit of the Beast, the noise of whose approach she expected to hear every instant. But the hour so much desired came without the appearance of the Beast. Alarmed, and almost angry at his delay, she tried in vain to account for his absence. Divided through hope and fear, her mind agitated, her heart a prey to melancholy, she descended into the gardens, determined not to re-enter the Palace till she had found the Beast.

No trace of him could she discover anywhere. She called him. Echo alone answered her. Having passed more than three hours in this disagreeable exercise, overcome by fatigue, she sank upon a garden seat.

She imagined the Beast was either dead or had abandoned the place. She saw herself alone in that Palace, without the hope of ever leaving it. She regretted her conversations with the Beast, un-entertaining as they had been to her, and what appeared to her extraordinary, even to discover she had so much feeling for him. She blamed herself for not having married him, and considering she had been the cause of his death (for she feared her too long absence had occasioned it), heaped upon herself the keenest and most bitter reproaches.

In the midst of her miserable reflections, she perceived that she was seated in that very avenue in which, during the last night she had passed under her father's roof, she had dreamed she saw the Beast expiring in some strange cavern.

Convinced that chance had not conducted her to this spot, she rose and hurried towards the thicket, which she found was not impenetrable. She discovered another hollow, which appeared to be that she had seen in her dream. As the moon gave but a feeble light, the monkey pages immediately appeared with a sufficient number of torches to illuminate the chasm, and to reveal to her the Beast stretched upon the earth, as she thought, asleep.

Far from being alarmed at his sight, Beauty was delighted, and, approaching him boldly, placed her hand upon his head, and called to him several times; but finding him cold and motionless, she no longer doubted he was dead, and consequently gave utterance to the most mournful shrieks and the most affecting exclamations.

The assurance of his death, however, did not prevent her from making every effort to recall him to life. On placing her hand on his heart she felt, to her great joy, that it still beat.

Without further delay, Beauty ran out of the cave to the basin of a fountain, where, taking up some water in her joined hands, she hastened back with it, and sprinkled it upon him; but as she could bring very little at a time, and spilt some of it before she could return to the Beast, her assistance had been but meagre if the monkey courtiers had not flown to the Palace, and returned with such speed that in a moment she was furnished with a vase for water, as well as with proper restoratives. She caused him to smell them and swallow them, and they produced so excellent an effect that he soon began to move and show some kind of consciousness. She cheered him with her voice and caressed him as he recovered.

"What anxiety have you caused me?" she said to him kindly. "I knew not how much I loved you. The fear of losing you has proved to me that I was attached to you by stronger ties than those of gratitude. I vow to you that I had determined to die if I had failed in restoring you to life."

At these tender words the Beast, feeling perfectly revived, replied, in a voice which was still feeble, "It is very kind of you, Beauty, to love so ugly a Beast, but you do well. I love you better than my life. I thought you would never return: it would have killed me. Since you love me I will live. Retire to rest, and assure yourself that you will be as happy as your good heart renders you worthy to be."

Beauty had never before heard so long a speech from the Beast. It was not very eloquent, but it pleased, from its gentleness and the sincerity observable in it. She had expected to be scolded, or at least to have been reproached. She had from this moment a better opinion of his disposition.

No longer thinking him so stupid, she even considered his short answers a proof of his prudence, and, more and more prepossessed in his favour, she retired to her apartment, her mind occupied with the most flattering ideas.

Extremely fatigued, she found there all the refreshments she needed. Her heavy eyelids promised her a sweet slumber. Asleep almost as soon as her head was on her pillow, her dear Unknown failed not to present himself immediately. What tender words did he not utter to express the pleasure he experienced at seeing her again? He assured her that she would be happy; that it only remained to her to follow the impulse of her good heart. Beauty asked him if her happiness was to arise from her marriage with the Beast. The Unknown replied that it was the only means of securing it. She felt somewhat annoyed at this. She thought it even extraordinary that her lover should advise her to make her rival happy.

After this first dream, she thought she saw the Beast dead at her feet. An instant afterwards, the Unknown reappeared and disappeared again as instantly, to give place to the Beast. But what she observed most distinctly was the Lady, who seemed to say to her, "I am pleased with you. Continue to follow the dictates of reason, and trouble yourself about naught. I undertake the task of rendering you happy."

Beauty, although asleep, appeared to acknowledge her partiality to the Unknown and her repugnance to the Beast, whom she could not consider loveable. The Lady smiled at her objections, and advised her not to make herself uneasy about her affection for the Unknown, for that the emotions she felt were not incompatible with the resolution she had formed to do her duty; that she might follow her inclinations without resistance, and that her happiness would be perfected by espousing the Beast.

This dream, which only ended with her sleep, furnished

her with an inexhaustible source of reflection. In this vision, as in those which had preceded it, she found more coherence than is usually displayed in dreams, and she therefore determined to consent to this strange union. But the image of the Unknown rose unceasingly to trouble her. It was the sole obstacle, but not a slight one. Still uncertain as to the course she ought to take, she went to the Opera, but without terminating her embarrassment. At the end of the performance she sat down to supper. The arrival of the Beast was alone capable of deciding her.

Far from reproaching her for her long absence, the Beast, as if the pleasure of seeing her had made him forget his past distresses, appeared, on entering Beauty's apartment, to have no other anxiety but that of ascertaining if she had been much amused, if she had been well received, and if her health had been good. She answered these questions, and added politely that she had paid dearly for all the pleasures his care had enabled her to enjoy, by the cruel pain she had endured on finding him in so sad a state on her return.

The Beast briefly thanked her, and then being about to take his leave, asked her, as usual, if she would marry him. Beauty was silent for a short time, but at last making up her mind, she said to him, trembling, "Yes, Beast, I am willing, if you will pledge me your faith, to give you mine."

"I do," the Beast replied, "and I promise you never to have any wife but you."

"Then," rejoined Beauty, "I accept you for my husband, and swear to be a fond and faithful wife to you." She had scarcely uttered these words when a discharge of artillery was heard, and that she might not doubt it being a signal of rejoicing, she saw from her windows the sky all in a blaze with the light of twenty thousand fireworks, which continued rising for three hours. They formed true-lovers' knots, while on elegant escutcheons appeared Beauty's initials, and beneath them, in well-defined letters, *'Long live Beauty and her Husband'*. After this display had terminated, the Beast took his departure, and Beauty retired to rest.

No sooner was she asleep than her dear Unknown paid her his usual visit. He was more richly attired than she had ever seen him. "How deeply am I obliged to you, charming Beauty," he said. "You have released me from the frightful prison in which I have groaned for so long a time. Your marriage with the Beast will restore a King to his subjects, a son to his mother, and life to a whole Kingdom. We shall all be happy."

Beauty, at these words, felt bitterly annoyed, perceiving that the Unknown, far from evincing the despair such an engagement as she had entered into should have caused him, gazed on her with eyes sparkling with extreme delight. She was about to express her discontent to him, when the Lady, in her turn, appeared in her dream.

"Behold you victorious," said she. "We owe everything to you, Beauty. You have suffered gratitude to triumph over every other feeling. None but you would have had the courage to keep their word at the expense of their inclination, nor to have periled their life to have saved that of their father. In return for this, there are none who can ever hope to enjoy such happiness as your virtue has won for you. You know at present little, but the rising sun shall tell you more."

When the Lady had disappeared, Beauty again saw the unknown youth, but stretched on the earth as dead. All the night passed in such dreams; but they had become familiar to her, and did not prevent her from sleeping long and soundly. It was broad daylight when she awoke. The sun streamed into her apartment with more brilliancy than usual: her monkeys had not closed the shutters.

Believing the sight that met her eyes but a continuation of her dreams, and that she was sleeping still, her joy and surprise were extreme at discovering that it was a reality, and that on a couch beside her lay, in a profound slumber, her beloved Unknown, looking a thousand times more handsome than he had done in her vision. To assure herself of the fact, she arose hastily and took from off her toilet-table the miniature she usually wore on her arm; but she could not have been mistaken.

She spoke to him, in the hope of awaking him from the trance into which he seemed to have been thrown by some wonderful power. Not stirring at her voice, she shook him by the arm. This effort was equally ineffectual, and only served to convince her that he was under the influence of enchantment, and that she must await the end of the charm, which it was reasonable to suppose had an appointed period.

How delighted was she to find herself betrothed to him who alone had caused her to hesitate, and to find that she had done from duty that which she would have done from inclination. She no longer doubted the promise of happiness which had been made to her in her dreams. She now knew that the Lady had truly assured her that her love for the Unknown was not incompatible with the affection she entertained for the Beast, seeing that they were one and the same person. In the meanwhile, however, her intended never woke.

CHAPTER VIII
UNEXPECTED GUESTS

After a slight meal, Beauty endeavoured to pass away the time in her usual occupations, but they appeared to her insipid. As she could not resolve to leave her apartments, nor bear to sit idle, she took up some music, and began to sing. Her birds hearing her, joined their voices to hers, and made a concert, the more charming to her as she expected every moment it would be interrupted by the awakening of her husband, for she flattered herself she could dissolve the spell by the harmony of her voice.

The spell was soon broken, but not by the means she imagined. She heard the sound of a chariot rolling beneath the windows of her apartment, and the voices of several persons approaching. At the same moment the monkey Captain of the Guard, by the beak of his parrot Interpreter, announced the visit of some ladies. Beauty, from her windows, beheld the chariot that brought them. It was of an entirely novel description, and of matchless beauty. Four white stags, with horns and hoofs of gold, superbly caparisoned, drew this equipage, the singularity of which increased Beauty's desire to know who the owners of it were.

By the noise, which became louder, she was aware that the ladies had nearly reached the antechamber. She considered it right to advance and receive them. She recognised in one of them the Lady she had been accustomed to behold in her dreams. The other was not less beautiful. Her high and distinguished bearing sufficiently indicated that she was an illustrious personage. She was no longer in the bloom of youth, but her air was so majestic that Beauty was uncertain to which of the two strangers she ought first to address herself.

She was still under this embarrassment, when the one with whose features she was already familiar, and who appeared to exercise some sort of superiority over the other, turning to her companion, said, "Well, Queen, what think you of this beautiful girl? You owe to her the restoration of your son to life, for you must admit that the miserable circumstances under which he existed could not be called living. Without her, you would never again have beheld this Prince. He must have remained in the horrible shape to which he had been transformed, had he not found in the world one only person who possessed virtue and courage equal to her beauty. I think you will behold with pleasure the son she has restored to you become her husband. They love each other, and nothing is wanting to their perfect happiness but your consent. Will you refuse to bestow it on them?"

The Queen, at these words, embracing Beauty affectionately, exclaimed, "Far from refusing my consent, their union will afford me the greatest felicity! Charming and virtuous child, to whom I am under so many obligations, tell me who you are, and the names of the sovereigns who are so happy as to have given birth to so perfect a Princess?"

"Madam," replied Beauty, modestly, "it is long since I had a mother; my father is a merchant more distinguished in the world for his probity and his misfortunes than for his birth."

At this frank declaration, the astonished Queen recoiled a pace or two, and said, "What! You are only a merchant's daughter? Ah, great Fairy!" she added, casting a mortified look on her companion, and then remained silent; but her manner sufficiently expressed her thoughts, and her disappointment was legible in her eyes.

"It appears to me," said the Fairy, haughtily, "that you are discontented with my choice. You regard with contempt the condition of this young person, and yet she was the only being in the world capable of executing my project and who could make your son happy."

"I am very grateful to her for what she has done," replied the Queen; "but, powerful spirit," she continued, "I cannot refrain from pointing out to you the incongruous mixture of that noblest blood in all the world which runs in my son's veins with that of the obscure race from which the person has sprung to whom you would unite him. I confess I am little gratified by the supposed happiness of the Prince, if it must be purchased by an alliance so degrading to us, and so unworthy of him. Is it impossible to find in the world a maiden whose birth is equal to her virtue? I know many excellent princesses by name; why am I not permitted to hope that I may see him the possessor of one of those?"

At this moment the handsome Unknown appeared. The arrival of his mother and the Fairy had aroused him, and the noise they had made was more effective than all the efforts of Beauty; such being the nature of the spell. The Queen held him a long time in her arms, without speaking a word. She found again a son whose fine qualities rendered him worthy of all her affection. What joy for the Prince to see himself released from a horrible form and a stupidity more painful to him because it was affected and had not obscured his reason. He had recovered the liberty to appear in his natural form by means of the object of his love, and that reflection made it still more precious to him.

After the first transports which nature inspired him with at the sight of his mother, the Prince hastened to pay those thanks to the Fairy which duty and gratitude prompted. He did so in the most respectful terms, but as briefly as possible, in order to be at liberty to turn his attentions towards Beauty.

He had already, by tender glances, expressed to her his feelings, and was about to confirm with his lips, in the most touching language, what his eyes had spoken, when the Fairy stopped him, and bade him be the judge between her and his mother.

"Your mother," she said, "condemns the engagement you have entered into with Beauty. She considers that her birth is too much beneath yours. For my part, I think that her virtues make up for that inequality. It is for you, Prince, to say with which of us your own feelings coincide; and that you may be under no restraint in declaring to us your real sentiments, I announce to you that you have full liberty of choice. Although you have pledged your word to this amiable person, you are free to withdraw it.

"I will answer for her, that Beauty will release you from your promise without the least hesitation, although, through her kindness, you have regained your natural form; and I assure you also that her generosity will cause her to carry disinterestedness to the extent of leaving you at liberty to dispose of your hand in favour of any person on whom the Queen may advise you to bestow it. What say you, Beauty?" pursued the Fairy, turning towards her. "Have I been mistaken in thus interpreting your sentiments? Would you desire a husband who would become so with regret?"

"Assuredly not, Madam," replied Beauty. "The Prince is free. I renounce the honour of being his wife. When I accepted him, I believed I was taking pity on something below humanity. I engaged myself to him only with the object of conferring on him the most signal favour. Ambition had no place in my thoughts. Therefore, great Fairy, I implore you to exact no sacrifice from the Queen, whom I cannot blame for the scruples she entertains under such circumstances."

"Well, Queen, what say you to that?" inquired the Fairy, in a disdainful and displeased tone. "Do you consider that princesses, who are so by the caprice of fortune, better deserve the high rank in which it has placed them than this young maiden? For my part, I think she should not be prejudiced by an origin from which she has elevated herself by her conduct."

The Queen replied with some embarrassment, "Beauty is incomparable! Her merit is infinite; nothing can surpass it; but, madam, can we not find some other mode of rewarding her? Is it not to be effected without sacrificing to her the hand of my son?" Then turning to Beauty, she continued, "Yes, I owe you more than I can pay. I put, therefore, no limit to your desires. Ask boldly, I will grant you everything, with that sole exception; but the difference will not be great to you. Choose a husband from amongst the nobles of my Court. However high in rank, he will have cause to bless his good fortune, and for your sake I will place him so near the throne that your position will be scarcely less enviable."

"I thank you, Madam," replied Beauty; "but I ask no reward from you. I am more than repaid by the pleasure of having broken the spell which had deprived a great prince of his mother and of his Kingdom. My happiness would have been perfect if I had rendered this service to my own sovereign. All I desire is that the Fairy will deign to restore me to my father."

The Prince, who, by order of the Fairy, had been silent throughout this conversation, was no longer master of himself, and his respect for the commands he had received, failed to restrain him. He flung himself at the feet of the Fairy and of his mother, and implored them, in the strongest terms, not to make him more miserable than he had been, by sending away Beauty, and depriving him of the happiness of being her husband.

At these words, Beauty, gazing on him with an air full of tenderness, but mingled with a noble pride, said, "Prince, I cannot conceal from you my affection. Your disenchantment is a proof of it, and I should in vain endeavour to disguise my feelings. I confess without a blush, that I love you better than myself. Why should I dissimulate? We may disavow evil impulses; but mine are perfectly innocent, and are authorised by the generous Fairy to whom we are both so much indebted. But if I could resolve to sacrifice my feelings when I thought it my duty to do so for the Beast, you must feel assured that I shall not falter on this occasion when it is no longer the interest of the Beast that is at stake, but your own.

"It is enough for me to know who you are, and that I am to renounce the glory of being your wife. I will even venture to say, that if, yielding to your entreaties, the Queen should grant the consent you ask, it would not alter the case, for in my own reason, and even in my love, you would meet with an insurmountable obstacle. I repeat that I ask no favour but that of being allowed to return to the bosom of my family, where I shall for ever cherish the remembrance of your bounty and your affection."

"Generous Fairy!" exclaimed the Prince, clasping her hands in supplication, "for mercy's sake, do not allow Beauty to depart! Make me, rather, again the Beast that I was, for then I shall be her husband. She pledged her word to the Beast, and I prefer that happiness to all those she has restored me to, if I must purchase them so dearly!"

The Fairy made no answer; she but looked steadily at the Queen, who was moved by so much true affection, but whose pride remained unshaken. The despair of her son affected her, yet she could not forget that Beauty was the daughter of a merchant, and nothing more. She, notwithstanding, feared the anger of the Fairy, whose manner and silence sufficiently evinced her indignation. Her confusion was extreme. Not having power to utter a word, she feared to see a fatal termination to a conference which had offended the protecting spirit.

No one spoke for some minutes, but the Fairy at length broke the silence, and casting an affectionate look upon the lovers, she said to them, "I find you worthy of each other. It would be a crime to part two such excellent persons. You shall not be separated, I promise you; and I have sufficient power to fulfil my promise."

The Queen shuddered at these words, and would have made some remonstrance, but the Fairy anticipated her by saying, "For you, Queen, the little value you set upon virtue, unadorned by the vain titles which alone you respect, would justify me in heaping on you the bitterest reproaches. But I excuse your fault, arising from pride of birth, and I will take no other vengeance beyond doing this little violence to your prejudices, and for which you will not be long without thanking me."

Beauty, at these words, embraced the knees of the Fairy, and exclaimed, "Ah, do not expose me to the misery of being told all my life that I am unworthy of the rank to which your bounty would elevate me. Reflect that this Prince, who now believes that his happiness consists in the possession of my hand, may very shortly perhaps be of the same opinion as the Queen."

"No, no, Beauty, fear nothing," rejoined the Fairy. "The evils you anticipate cannot come to pass. I know a sure way of protecting you from them, and should the Prince be capable of despising you after marriage, he must seek some other reason than the inequality of your condition. Your birth is not inferior to his own. Nay, the advantage is even considerably on your side, for the truth is," she said sternly to the Queen, "that you behold your niece; and what must render her still more worthy of your respect is that she is mine also, being the daughter of my sister, who was not, like you, a slave to rank which is lustreless without virtue.

"That Fairy, knowing how to estimate true worth, did your brother, the King of the Fortunate Island, the honour to marry him. I preserved this fair fruit of their union from the fury of a Fairy who desired to be her stepmother. From the moment of her birth, I destined her to be the wife of your son. I desired, by concealing from you the result of my good service, to give you an opportunity of showing your confidence in me. I had some reason to believe that it was greater than it appears to have been. You might have relied upon me for watching over the destiny of the Prince. I had given you proofs enough of the interest I took in it, and you needed not to have been under any apprehension that I should expose him to anything that would be disgraceful to him or to you. I feel persuaded, Madam," continued she, with a smile which had still something of bitterness in it, "that you will not object to honour us with your alliance."

The Queen, astonished and embarrassed, knew not what to answer. The only way to atone for her fault was to confess it frankly, and evince a sincere repentance. "I am guilty, generous Fairy," she said. "Your bounties should have satisfied me that you would not suffer my son to have formed an alliance unworthy of him. But pardon, I beseech you, the prejudices of my rank, which urged that royal blood could not marry one of humbler birth without degradation. I acknowledge that I deserve you should punish me by giving to Beauty a mother-in-law more worthy of her; but you take too kind an interest in my son to render him the victim of my error.

"As to you, dear Beauty," she continued, embracing her tenderly, "you must not resent my resistance. It was caused by my desire to marry my son to my niece, whom the Fairy had often assured me was living, notwithstanding all appearances to the contrary. She had drawn so charming a portrait of her, that without knowing you, I loved you dearly enough to risk offending the Fairy, in order to preserve to you the throne and the heart of my son." So saying, she recommenced her caresses, which Beauty received with respect.

The Prince, on his part, enraptured at this agreeable intelligence, expressed his delight in looks alone.

"Behold us all satisfied," said the Fairy; "and now, to terminate this happy adventure, we only need the consent of the royal father of the Princess; but we shall shortly see him here."

Beauty requested her to permit the person who had brought her up, and whom she had up till now looked upon as her father, to witness her felicity. "I admire such consideration," said the Fairy; "it is worthy a noble mind, and as you desire it, I undertake to inform him." Then taking the Queen by the hand, she led her away, under the pretext of showing her over the enchanted Palace. It was to give the newly-betrothed pair the liberty of conversing with each other for the first time without restraint or the aid of illusion. They would have followed, but she forbade them.

CHAPTER IX
REVELATIONS OF THE PAST

The happiness in store for Beauty and the Prince inspired each with equal delight. They could not entertain the least doubt of their mutual affection. Their conversation, confused and unconnected, their protestations a hundred times repeated, were to them more convincing proofs of love than the most eloquent language could have afforded. After having exhausted all the expressions that passion suggests under such circumstances to those that are truly in love, Beauty inquired of her lover by what misfortune he had been so cruelly transformed into a beast. She requested him also to relate to her all the events of his life preceding that shocking metamorphosis.

The Prince, whose recovery of his natural form had not lessened his anxiety to obey her, without more ado commenced his narrative in the following words: "The King, my father, died before I was born. The Queen would never have been consoled for his loss if her interest for the child she bore had not struggled with her sorrow. My birth caused her extreme delight. The sweet task of rearing the fruit of the affection of so dearly beloved a husband was destined to dissipate her affliction. The care of my education and the fear of losing me occupied her entirely. She was assisted in her object by a Fairy of her acquaintance, who showed the greatest anxiety to preserve me from all kinds of accidents. The Queen felt greatly obliged to her, but she was not pleased when the Fairy asked her to place me entirely in her hands. The Fairy had not the best of reputations she was said to be capricious in her favours. People feared more than they loved her; and even had my mother been perfectly convinced of the goodness of her nature, she could not have resolved to lose sight of me.

"By the advice, however, of prudent persons, and for fear of suffering from the fatal effects of the resentment of this vindictive Fairy, she did not flatly refuse her. If voluntarily confided to her care there was no reason to suppose she would do me any injury. Experience had proved that she took pleasure in hurting those only by whom she considered herself offended. The Queen admitted this, and was only reluctant to forego the pleasure of gazing on me continually with a mother's eyes, which enabled her to discover charms in me I owed solely to her partiality.

"She was still irresolute as to the course she should adopt, when a powerful neighbour imagined it would be an easy matter for him to seize upon the dominions of an infant governed by a woman. He invaded my Kingdom with a formidable army. The Queen hastily raised one to oppose him, and, with courage beyond that of her sex, placed herself at the head of her troops, and marched to defend our frontiers.

"It was then that, being compelled to leave me, she could not avoid confiding to the Fairy the care of my education. I was placed in her hands after she had sworn by all she held most sacred that she would, without the least hesitation, bring me back to the Court as soon as the war was over, which my mother calculated would not last more than a year at the utmost. Notwithstanding, however, all the advantages she gained over the enemy, she found it impossible to return to the capital as soon as she expected. To profit by her victory, after having driven the foe out of our dominions, she pursued him in his own.

"She took entire provinces, gained battle after battle, and finally reduced the vanquished to sue for a degrading peace, which he obtained only on the hardest conditions. After this glorious success, the Queen returned triumphantly, and enjoyed in anticipation the pleasure of beholding me once more; but having learned upon her march that her base foe, in violation of the treaty, had surprised and massacred our garrisons, and repossessed himself of nearly all the places he had been compelled to cede to us, she was obliged to retrace her steps.

"Honour prevailed over the affection which drew her towards me, and she resolved never to sheathe the sword till she had put it out of her enemy's power to perpetrate more treachery. The time employed in this second expedition was very considerable. She had flattered herself that two or three campaigns would suffice; but she had to contend with an adversary as cunning as he was false. He contrived to excite rebellion in some of our own provinces, and to corrupt entire battalions, which forced the Queen to remain in arms for fifteen years. She never thought of sending for me. She was always flattering herself that each month would be the last she should be absent, and that she was on the point of seeing me again.

"In the meanwhile, the Fairy, in accordance with her promise, had paid every attention to my education. From the day she had taken me out of my Kingdom, she had never left me, nor ceased to give me proof of the interest she felt in all that concerned my health and amusement. I evinced by my respect for her how sensible I was of her kindness. I showed her the same deference, the same attention that I should have shown to my mother, and gratitude inspired me with as much affection for her.

"For some time she appeared satisfied with my behaviour; but one day, without imparting to me the motive, she set out on a journey, from which she did not return for some years, and when she did return, struck with the effect of her care of me, she conceived for me an affection differing from that of a mother. She had previously permitted me to call her by that name, but now she forbade me. I obeyed her without inquiring what were her reasons, or suspecting what she was about to exact from me.

"I saw clearly that she was dissatisfied; but could I imagine why she continually complained of my ingratitude? I was the more surprised at her reproaches as I did not feel I deserved them. They were always followed or preceded by the most tender caresses. I was not old enough to comprehend her. She was compelled to explain herself.

"She did so one day when I evinced some sorrow, mingled with impatience, respecting the continued absence of the Queen. She reproached me for this, and on my assuring her that my affection for my mother in no way interfered with that I owed to her, she replied that she was not jealous, although she had done so much for me, and had resolved to do still more; but that, to enable her to carry out her designs in my favour with greater freedom, it was requisite, she added, that I should marry her; that she did not desire to be loved by me as a mother, but as an admirer; that she had no doubt of my gratitude to her for making this proposal, or of the great joy with which I should accept it, and that, consequently, I had only to abandon myself to the delight with which the certainty of becoming the husband of a powerful Fairy, who could protect me from all dangers, assure me an existence full of happiness, and cover me with glory, must naturally awaken.

"I was sadly embarrassed by this proposition. I knew enough of the world in my own country, to be aware that amongst the wedded portion of the community the happiest were those whose ages and characters assimilated, and that many were much to be pitied who, marrying under opposite circumstances, had found antipathies existing between them which were the source of constant misery.

"The Fairy being old and of a haughty disposition, I could not flatter myself that my lot would be as agreeable as she predicted. I was far from entertaining for her such feelings as one should for the woman with whom we intend to pass our days; and besides, I was not inclined to enter into any such engagement at so early an age. My only desire was to see the Queen again, and to signalize myself at the head of her forces. I sighed for liberty; that was the sole boon that would have gratified me, and the only one the Fairy would not grant.

"I had often implored her to allow me to share the perils to which I knew the Queen exposed herself for the protection of my interests, but my prayers had up till now been fruitless. Pressed to reply to the astounding declaration she had made to me, I in some confusion, recalled to her that she had often told me that I had no right to dispose of my hand without the commands of my mother, and in her absence. 'That is exactly my opinion,' she replied. 'I do not wish you to do otherwise; I am satisfied that you should refer the matter to the Queen.'

"I have already informed you, beautiful Princess, that I had been unable to obtain from the Fairy permission to seek the Queen, my mother. The desire she now had to receive her sanction, which she never doubted she should obtain, obliged her to grant, even without my asking, that which she had always denied me; but it was on the condition, by no means agreeable to me, that she should accompany me. I did what I could to dissuade her, but found it impossible, and we set out together with a numerous escort. We arrived upon the eve of a decisive action. The Queen had manoeuvred with such skill that the next day was certain to decide the fate of the enemy, who would have no resource if he lost the battle.

"My presence created great pleasure in the camp, and gave additional courage to our troops, who drew a favourable augury from my arrival. The Queen was ready to die with joy; but this first transport of delight was succeeded by the greatest alarm. Whilst I exulted in the hope of acquiring glory, the Queen trembled at the danger to which I was about to expose myself - too generous to endeavour to prevent me. She implored me by all her affection, to take as much care of myself as honour would permit, and entreated the Fairy not to abandon me on that occasion.

"Her solicitations were unnecessary. The too susceptible Fairy was as much alarmed as the Queen, for she possessed no spell which could protect me from the chances of war. However, by instantly inspiring me with the art of commanding an army, and the prudence requisite for so important an office, she achieved much. The most experienced captains were surprised at me. I remained master of the field. The victory was complete. I had the happiness of saving the Queen's life, and of preventing her from being made prisoner of war.

"The enemy was pursued with such vigour that he abandoned his camp, lost his baggage, and more than three-fourths of his army, while the loss on our side was inconsiderable. A slight wound which I had received was the only advantage the foe could boast of; but the Queen, fearing that if the war continued some more serious mischief might befall me, in opposition to the desire of the whole army, to which my presence had imparted fresh spirit, made peace on more advantageous terms than the vanquished had ventured to hope for.

"A short time afterwards we returned to our capital, which we entered in triumph. My occupation during the war, and the continual presence of my ancient adorer, had prevented me from informing the Queen of what had occurred. She was, therefore, completely taken by surprise when the Fairy told her, in so many words, that she had determined to marry me immediately. This declaration was made in this very Palace, but which was at that time not as superb as it is at present. It had been a country residence of the late King, which a thousand occupations had prevented his embellishing. My mother, who cherished everything that he had loved, had selected it in preference to any other as a place of retirement after the fatigues of the war.

"At the avowal of the Fairy, unable to control her first feelings, and unused to dissemble, she exclaimed, 'Have you reflected, Madam, on the absurdity of the arrangement you propose to me!'

"In truth it was impossible to conceive one more ridiculous. In addition to the almost decrepit old age of the Fairy, she was horribly ugly. Nor was this the effect of time. If she had been handsome in her youth, she might have preserved some portion of her beauty by the aid of her art; but naturally hideous, her power could only invest her with the appearance of beauty for one day in each year, and that day ended, she returned to her former state.

"The Fairy was surprised at the exclamation of the Queen. Her self-love concealed from her all that was actually horrible in her person, and she calculated that her power sufficiently compensated for the loss of a few charms of her youth. 'What do you mean,' said she to the Queen, 'by an absurd arrangement! Consider, that it is imprudent in you to make me remember what I have condescended to forget. You ought only to congratulate yourself on possessing a son so amiable that his merit induces me to prefer him to the most powerful Fairy in all the elements; and as I have deigned to descend to him, accept with respect the honour I am good enough to confer on you, and do not give me time to change my mind.'

"The Queen, as proud as the Fairy, had never conceived that there was a rank on earth higher than the throne. She valued little the pretended honour which the Fairy offered her. Having always commanded everyone who approached her, she by no means desired to have a daughter-in-law to whom she must herself pay homage. Therefore, far from replying to her, she remained motionless, and contented herself with fixing her eyes upon me.

"I was as much astounded as she was, and fixing my eyes on her in the same manner, it was easy for the Fairy to perceive that our silence expressed sentiments very opposite to the joy with which she would have inspired us. 'What is the meaning of this?' she said sharply. 'How comes it that mother and son are both silent? Has this agreeable surprise deprived you of the power of speech? Or are you blind and rash enough to reject my offer? Say, Prince,' said she to me, 'are you so ungrateful and so imprudent as to despise my kindness? Do you not consent to give me your hand this moment?'

"'No, Madam, I assure you,' I replied quickly. 'Although I am sincerely grateful to you for past favours, I cannot agree to discharge my debt to you by such means; and, with the Queen's permission, I decline to part so soon with my liberty. Name any other mode of acknowledging your favours and I will not consider it impossible; but as to that you have proposed, excuse me if you please.'

"'How! Insignificant creature!' interrupted the Fairy, furiously. 'You dare to resist me! And you, foolish Queen! You see, without anger, this conduct - what do I say? Without anger! It is you who authorize it! For it is your own insolent looks that have inspired him with the audacity to refuse me!'

"The Queen, already stung by the contemptuous language of the Fairy, was no longer mistress of herself, and accidentally casting her eyes on a looking-glass, before which we happened to be standing at the moment, the wicked Fairy thus provoked her: 'What answer can I make you,' she said, 'that you ought not to make to yourself? Deign to contemplate, without prejudice, the object this glass presents to you, and let it reply for me.'

"The Fairy easily comprehended the Queen's insinuation. 'It is the beauty, then, of this precious son of yours that renders you so vain,' she said to her, 'and has exposed me to so degrading a refusal! I appear to you unworthy of him. Well,' she continued, raising her voice furiously, 'having taken so many pains to make him charming, it is fit that I should complete my work and that I should give you both a cause, as novel as remarkable, to make you remember what you owe to me. Go, wretch!' she said to me; 'boast that you have refused my heart and my hand. Give them to her you find more worthy of them than I am.'

"So saying, my terrible lover struck me a blow on the head. It was so heavy that I was dashed to the ground on my face, and felt as though I were crushed by the fall of a mountain. Irritated by this insult, I struggled to rise, but found it impossible. The weight of my body had become so great that I could not lift myself; all that I could do was to sustain myself on my hands, which had in an instant become two horrible paws, and the sight of them apprised me of the change I had undergone. My form was that in which you found me. I cast my eyes for an instant on that fatal glass, and could no longer doubt my cruel and sudden transformation.

"My despair rendered me motionless. The Queen at this dreadful sight was almost out of her mind. To put the last seal upon her barbarity, the furious Fairy said to me, in an ironical tone, 'Go make illustrious conquests, more worthy of you than an august Fairy. And as sense is not required when one is so handsome, I command you to appear as stupid as you are horrible, and to remain in this state until a young and beautiful girl shall, of her own accord, come to seek you, although fully persuaded you will devour her.

"'She must also,' continued the Fairy, 'after discovering that her life is not in danger, conceive for you a sufficiently tender affection to induce her to marry you. Until you can meet with this rare maiden, it is my pleasure that you remain an object of horror to yourself and to all who behold you. As for you, too happy mother of so lovely a child,' said she to the Queen, 'I warn you that if you acknowledge to anyone that this Beast is your son, he shall never recover his natural shape. Neither interest, nor ambition, nor the charms of his conversation, must assist to restore him to it. *Adieu!* Do not be impatient; you will not have long to wait. Such a darling will soon find a remedy for his misfortune.'

"'Ah, cruel one!' the Queen exclaimed, 'if my refusal has offended you, let your vengeance light on me. Take my life, but do not, I conjure you, destroy your own work.'

"'You forget yourself, great Princess,' replied the Fairy, in an ironical tone, 'you demean yourself too much. I am not handsome enough for you to condescend to entreat me; but I am firm in my resolutions. *Adieu*, powerful Queen; *adieu*, beautiful Prince; it is not fair that I should longer annoy you with my hateful presence. I withdraw; but I have still charity enough to warn you,' she said, addressing me, 'that you must forget who you are. If you suffer yourself to be flattered by vain respects or by pompous titles, you are lost irretrievably! And you are equally lost if you should dare to avail yourself of the intellect I leave you possessed of to shine in conversation.'

"With these words she disappeared, and left the Queen and me in a state which can neither be described nor imagined. Lamentations are the consolation of the unhappy; but our misery was too great to seek relief in them. My mother determined to stab herself, and I to fling myself in the adjacent canal. Without communicating our intentions to each other, we were on the point of executing these fatal designs, when a female of majestic mien, and whose manner inspired us with profound respect, appeared, and bade us remember that it was cowardice to succumb to the greatest misfortunes, and that with time and courage there was no evil that could not be remedied.

The Queen, however, was inconsolable; tears streamed from her eyes, and not knowing how to inform her subjects that their sovereign was transformed into a horrible Beast, she abandoned herself to the most fearful despair. The Fairy (for she was one, and the same whom you have seen here), knowing both her misery and her embarrassment, recalled to her the indispensable obligation she was under to conceal from her people this dreadful adventure, and that in lieu of yielding to despair, it would be better to seek some remedy for the mischief. 'Is there one to be found,' exclaimed the Queen, 'which is powerful enough to prevent the fulfilment of a Fairy's sentence?'

"'Yes, Madam,' replied the Fairy, 'there is a remedy for everything. I am a Fairy as well as she, whose fury you have just felt the effects of, and my power is equal to hers. It is true that I cannot immediately repair the injury she has done you, for we are not permitted to act directly in opposition to each other. She who has caused your misfortune is older than I am, and age has amongst us a particular title to respect. But as she could not avoid attaching a condition upon which the spell might be broken, I will assist you to break it. I grant that it will be a difficult task to terminate this enchantment; but it does not appear to me to be impossible. Let me see what I can do for you by the exertion of all the means in my power.'

"Upon this she drew a book from under her robe, and after taking a few mysterious steps, she seated herself at a table, and read for a considerable time with such intense application that large drops of perspiration stood on her forehead. At length, she closed the book and meditated profoundly.

"The expression of her countenance was so serious that for some time we were led to believe that she considered my misfortune irreparable; but recovering from a sort of trance, and her features resuming their natural beauty, she informed us that she had discovered a remedy for our disasters. 'It will be slow,' she said, 'but it will be sure. Keep your secret; let it not transpire, so that anyone can suspect you are concealed beneath this horrible disguise, for in that case you will deprive me of the power of delivering you from it. Your enemy flatters herself you will divulge it; it is for that reason she did not take from you the power of speech.'

"The Queen declared that the condition was an impossible one, as two of her women had been present at the fatal transformation, and had rushed out of the apartment in great terror, which must have excited the curiosity of the guards and the courtiers. She imagined that the whole Court was by this time aware of it, and that all the Kingdom, and even all the world, would speedily receive the intelligence; but the Fairy knew a way to prevent the disclosure of the secret.

"She made several circles, now solemnly, now rapidly, uttering words of which we could not comprehend the meaning, and finished by raising her hand in the air in the style of one who is pronouncing an imperative order. This gesture, added to the words she had uttered, was so powerful, that every breathing creature in the Palace became motionless, and was changed into a statue. They are all still in the same state. They are the figures you behold in various directions and in the very attitudes they had assumed at the instant the Fairy's potent spell surprised them.

"The Queen, who at that moment cast her eyes upon the great courtyard, observed this change taking place in a prodigious number of persons. The silence which suddenly succeeded to the stir of a multitude, awoke a feeling of compassion in her heart for the many innocent beings who were deprived of life for my sake; but the Fairy comforted her by saying that she would only retain her subjects in that condition as long as their discretion was necessary.

"It was a precaution she was compelled to take, but she promised she would make up to them for it, and that the period they passed in that state would not be added to the years allotted to their existence. 'They will be so much the younger,' said the Fairy to the Queen, 'so cease to deplore them, and leave them here with your son. He will be quite safe, for I have raised such thick fogs around this Palace, that it will be impossible for anyone to enter it but when we think fit. I will convey you,' she continued, 'where your presence is necessary. Your enemies are plotting against you. Be careful to proclaim to your people that the Fairy who educated your son retains him near her for an important purpose, and keeps with her also all the persons who were in attendance on you.'

"It was not without shedding a flood of tears that my mother could force herself to leave me. The Fairy renewed her assurances to her that she would always watch over me, and protested that I had only to wish, and to see the accomplishment of my desires. She added that my misfortunes would shortly end, provided neither the Queen nor I raised an obstacle by some act of imprudence. All these promises could not console my mother. She wished to remain with me and to leave the Fairy, or anyone she might consider the most proper person, to govern the Kingdom; but Fairies are imperious, and will be obeyed.

"My mother, fearing by a refusal to increase my miseries and deprive me of the aid of this beneficent spirit, consented to all she insisted on. She saw a beautiful carriage approach; it was drawn by the same white stags that brought her here today. The Fairy made the Queen mount by her side. She had scarcely time to embrace me, her affairs demanded her presence elsewhere, and she was warned that a longer sojourn in this place would be prejudicial to me. She was transported with extraordinary velocity to the spot where her army was encamped.

"They were not surprised to see her arrive with this equipage. Everybody believed her to be accompanied by the old Fairy, for the one who was with her kept herself unseen, and departed again immediately to return to this place, which, in an instant, she embellished with everything that her imagination could suggest and her art supply.

"This good-natured Fairy permitted me also to add whatever I fancied would please me, and after having done for me all she could, she left me with exhortations to take courage and promising to come occasionally and impart to me such hopes as she might entertain of a favourable issue to my adventure.

"I seemed to be alone in the Palace. I was only so to sight. I was served as if I was in the midst of my courtiers, and my occupations were nearly the same as those which were afterwards yours. I read, I went to the play, I cultivated a garden which I had made to amuse me, and found something agreeable in everything I undertook. What I planted arrived at perfection in the same day. It took no more time to produce the bower of roses to which I am indebted for the happiness of beholding you here.

"My benefactress came very often to see me. Her presence and her promises alleviated my distresses. Through her, the Queen received news of me, and I news of the Queen. One day I saw the Fairy arrive with joy sparkling in her eyes. 'Dear Prince,' she said to me, 'the moment of your happiness approaches!'

"She then informed me that he whom you believed to be your father had passed a very uncomfortable night in the forest. She related to me, in a few words, the adventure which had caused him to undertake the journey, without revealing to me your real parentage. She apprised me that the worthy man was compelled to seek an asylum from the misery he had endured during four-and-twenty hours.

"'I go,' she said, 'to give orders for his reception. It must be an agreeable one. He has a charming daughter. I propose that she shall release you. I have examined the conditions which my cruel companion has attached to your disenchantment. It is fortunate that she did not ordain that your deliverer should come here out of love for you. On the contrary, she insisted that the young maiden should expect no less than death, and yet expose herself to it voluntarily. I have thought of a scheme to oblige her to take that step. It is to make her believe the life of her father is in danger, and that she has no other means of saving him.

"'I know that in order to spare her father any expense on her account, she has asked him only to bring her a rose, while her sisters have overwhelmed him with extravagant commissions. He will naturally avail himself of the first favourable opportunity. Hide yourself in this arbour, and seizing him the instant he attempts to gather your roses, threaten him that death will be the punishment of his audacity, unless he give you one of his daughters; or, rather, unless she sacrifice herself, according to the decree of our enemy. This man has five daughters besides the one I have destined for you; but not one of them is sufficiently magnanimous to purchase the life of their father at the price of their own. Beauty is alone capable of so grand an action.'

"I executed exactly the Fairy's commands. You know, lovely Princess, with what success. The merchant, to save his life, promised what I demanded. I saw him depart without being able to persuade myself that he would return with you. I could not flatter myself that my desire would be fulfilled. What torment did I not suffer during the month he had requested me to allow him. I longed for its termination only to be certain of my disappointment. I could not imagine that a young, lovely, and amiable girl would have the courage to seek a Beast, of whom she believed she was doomed to be the prey. Even supposing her to have sufficient fortitude to devote herself, she would have to remain with me without repenting the step she had taken, and that appeared to me an invincible obstacle. Besides, how could she behold me without dying with affright?

"I passed my miserable existence in these melancholy reflections, and never was I more to be pitied. The month, however, elapsed, and my protectress announced to me your arrival. You remember, no doubt, the pomp with which you were received. Not daring to express my delight in words, I endeavoured to prove it to you by the most magnificent signs of rejoicing. The Fairy, ceaseless in her attentions to me, prohibited me from making myself known to you. Whatever terror I might inspire you with, or whatever kindness you might show me, I was not permitted to seek to please you, nor to express any love for you, nor to discover to you in any way who I was. I could have recourse, however, to excessive good nature, as, fortunately, the malignant Fairy had forgotten to forbid my giving you proof of that.

"These regulations seemed hard to me, but I was compelled to subscribe to them, and I resolved to present myself before you only for a few moments every day, and to avoid long conversations, in which my heart might betray its tenderness. You came, charming Princess, and the first sight of you produced upon me a diametrically opposite effect to that which my monstrous appearance must have done upon you. To see you was instantly to love you. Entering your apartment, tremblingly, my joy was excessive to find that you could behold me with greater intrepidity than I could behold myself. You delighted me infinitely when you declared that you would remain with me. An impulse of self-love, which I retained even under that most horrible of forms, led me to believe that you had not found me so hideous as you anticipated.

"Your father departed satisfied. But my sorrow increased as I reflected that I was not allowed to win your favour in any way except by indulging the caprices of your taste. Your demeanour, your conversation, as sensible as it was unpretending, everything in you convinced me that you acted solely on the principles dictated to you by reason and virtue, and that consequently I had nothing to hope for from a fortunate caprice. I was in despair at being forbidden to address you in any other language than that which the Fairy had dictated, and which she had expressly chosen as coarse and stupid.

"In vain did I represent to her it was unnatural to expect you would accept my proposition to marry you. Her answer was always, 'Patience, perseverance, or all is lost.' To recompense you for my silly conversation, she assured me she would surround you with all sorts of pleasures, and give me the advantage of seeing you continually, without alarming you, or being compelled to say rude and impertinent things to you. She rendered me invisible, and I had the gratification of seeing you waited on by spirits who were also invisible, or who presented themselves to you in the shapes of various animals.

"More than this, the Fairy caused you to behold my natural form in your nightly slumbers, and in portraits by day, and made it speak to you in your dreams as I should have spoken to you myself. You obtained a confused idea of my secret and my hopes, which she urged you to realize, and by the means of a starry mirror I witnessed all your interviews, and read in it either all you imagined you uttered or all that you actually thought. This position, however, did not suffice to render me happy. I was only so in a dream, and my sufferings were real.

"The intense affection with which you had inspired me obliged me to complain of the restraint under which I lived; but my state was much more wretched when I perceived that these beautiful scenes had no longer any charms for you. I saw you shed tears, which pierced my heart, and would have destroyed me. You asked me if I was alone here, and I was on the verge of discarding my feigned stupidity, and assuring you by the most passionate vows of the fact. They would have been uttered in terms that would have surprised you, and caused you to suspect that I was not so coarse a brute as I pretended to be.

"I was on the point even of declaring myself, when the Fairy, invisible to you, appeared before me. By a threatening gesture, which terrified me, she found a way to close my lips. O, heavens! By what means did she impose silence upon me? She approached you with a poniard in her hand, and made signs to me that the first word I uttered would cost you your life. I was so frightened that I naturally relapsed into the stupidity she had ordered me to affect.

"My sufferings were not yet at an end. You expressed a desire to visit your father. I gave you permission without hesitation. Could I have refused you anything? But I regarded your departure as my deathblow, and without the assistance of the Fairy I must have sunk under it. During your absence that generous being never quitted me. She saved me from destroying myself, which I should have done in my despair, not daring to hope that you would return. The time you had passed in this Palace rendered my condition more insupportable than it had been previously, because I felt I was the most miserable of all men, without the hope of making it known to you.

"My most agreeable occupation was to wander through the scenes which you had frequented, but my grief was increased by no longer seeing you there. The evenings and hours when I used to have the pleasure of conversing with you for a moment, redoubled my afflictions, and were still more painful to me. Those two months, the longest I had ever known, ended at last, and you did not return. It was then my misery reached its climax, and that the Fairy's power was too weak to prevent my sinking under my despair.

"The precautions she took to prevent my attempting my life were useless. I had a sure way which eluded her power. It was to refrain from food. By the potency of her spells she contrived to sustain me for some time, but having exhausted all her secrets, I grew weaker and weaker, and finally had but a few moments to breathe, when you arrived to snatch me from the tomb. Your precious tears, more efficacious than all the cordials of the disguised Genii who attended on me, delayed my soul upon the point of flight. In learning from your lamentations that I was clear to you, I enjoyed perfect felicity, and that felicity was at its height when you accepted me for your husband.

"Still I was not permitted to divulge to you my secret, and the Beast was compelled to leave you without daring to disclose to you the Prince. You know the lethargy into which I fell, and which ended only with the arrival of the Fairy and the Queen. On awaking I found myself as you behold me, without being aware of how the change took place.

"You have witnessed what followed, but you could only imperfectly judge of the pain which the obstinacy of my mother caused me in opposing a marriage so suitable and so glorious for me. I had determined, Princess, rather to be a Beast again than to abandon the hope of being the husband of so virtuous and charming a maiden. Had the secret of your birth remained for ever a mystery to me, love and gratitude would not less have assured me that in possessing you I was the most fortunate of men!"

The Prince thus ended his narration and Beauty was about to speak, when she was prevented by a burst of loud voices and warlike instruments.

CHAPTER X
ROYALTY FROM THE FORTUNATE ISLAND

The Prince and Princess looked out of the window, as did also the Fairy and the Queen who returned from their promenade. The noise was occasioned by the arrival of a personage who, according to all appearances, could be no less than a King. His escort was obviously a royal one, and there was an air of majesty in his demeanour which accorded with the state that accompanied him.

The fine form of this sovereign, although of a certain age, testified that there had been few who could have equalled him in appearance when in the flower of his youth. He was followed by twelve of his bodyguard, and some courtiers in hunting-dresses, who appeared as much astonished as their master to find themselves in a palace till now quite unknown to them. He was received with the same honours that would have been paid to him in his own dominions, and all by invisible beings. Shouts of joy and flourishes of trumpets were heard, but no one was to be seen.

The Fairy, immediately on beholding him, said to the Queen, "Here is the King your brother, and the father of Beauty. He little expects the pleasure of seeing you both here. He will be so much the more gratified, as you know he believes that his daughter has been long dead. He mourns her still, as he also does his wife, of whom he retains an affectionate remembrance."

These words increased the impatience of the Queen and the young Princess to embrace this monarch. They reached the courtyard just as he dismounted. He saw, but could not recognize them; not doubting, however, that they were advancing to receive him, he was considering how and in what terms he should pay his compliments to them, when Beauty, flinging herself at his feet, embraced his knees, and called him, "Father!"

The King raised her and pressed her tenderly in his arms, without comprehending why she addressed him by that title. He imagined she must be some orphan Princess, who sought his protection from some oppressor, and who made use of the most touching expression in order to obtain her request.

He was about to assure her that he would do all that lay in his power to assist her, when he recognized the Queen, his sister, who, embracing him in her turn, presented her son to him. She then informed him of some of the obligations they were under to Beauty, and especially of the frightful enchantment that had just been terminated. The King praised the young Princess, and desired to know her name, when the Fairy, interrupting him, asked if it was necessary to name her parents, and if he had never known anyone whom she resembled sufficiently to enable him to guess them.

"If I judged only from her features," he said, gazing upon her earnestly, and not being able to restrain a few tears, "the title she has given to me is legitimately my due; but notwithstanding that evidence, and the emotion which her presence occasions me, I dare not flatter myself that she is the daughter whose loss I have deplored; for I had the most positive proof that she had been devoured by wild beasts. Yet," he continued, still examining her countenance, "she resembles perfectly the tender and incomparable wife whom death has deprived me of. Oh, that I could but venture to indulge in the delightful hope of beholding again in her the fruit of a happy union, the bonds of which were too soon broken!"

"You may, my liege," replied the Fairy, "Beauty is your daughter. Her birth is no longer a secret here. The Queen and Prince know who she is. I caused you to direct your steps this way on purpose to inform you; but this is not a fitting place for me to enter into the details of this adventure. Let us enter the Palace. After you have rested yourself there a short time I will relate to you all you desire to know. When you have indulged in the delight which you must feel at finding a daughter so beautiful and so virtuous I will communicate to you another piece of intelligence, which will afford you equal gratification."

The King, accompanied by his daughter and the Prince, was ushered by the monkey officers into the apartment destined for him by the Fairy, who took this opportunity of restoring to the statues the liberty of relating what they had witnessed. As their fate had excited the compassion of the Queen, it was from her hands that the Fairy desired they should receive the benefit of reanimation. She placed her wand in the Queen's hand, who, by her instructions, described with it seven circles in the air, and then pronounced these words: "Be reanimated. Your King is restored to you." All the statues immediately began to move, walk, and act as formerly, retaining only a confused idea of what had happened to them.

After this ceremony, the Fairy and the Queen returned to the King, whom they found in conversation with Beauty and the Prince, caressing each in turn, and most fondly his daughter, of whom he inquired a hundred times how she had been preserved from the wild beasts who had carried her off, without remembering that she had answered him from the first that she knew nothing about it, and had been ignorant even of the secret of her birth.

The Prince also talked without being attended to, repeating a hundred times the obligations he was under to Princess Beauty. He desired to acquaint the King with the promises which the Fairy had made him, that he should marry the Princess, and to beg he would not refuse his cheerful consent to the alliance. This conversation and these caresses were interrupted by the entrance of the Queen and the Fairy. The King, who had recovered his daughter, fully appreciated his happiness, but was as yet ignorant, to whom he was indebted for this precious gift.

"It is to I," said the Fairy, "and I alone can explain to you the adventure. I shall not limit my benefits to the recital of that alone. I have other tidings in store for you, not less agreeable. Therefore, great King, you may note this day as one of the happiest of your life."

The company, perceiving that the Fairy was about to commence her narration, evinced by their silence the great attention they were anxious to pay to it. To satisfy their curiosity the Fairy thus addressed the King: "Beauty, my liege, and perhaps the Prince, are the only persons present who are not acquainted with the laws of the Fortunate Island. It is necessary I should explain those laws to them.

"The inhabitants of that island, and even the King himself, are allowed perfect liberty to marry according to their inclinations, in order that there may be no obstacle whatever to their happiness. It was in virtue of this privilege that you, Sire, selected for your wife a young shepherdess whom you met one day when you were hunting. Her beauty and her good conduct were considered by you deserving of that honour. You raised her to the throne, and placed her in a rank from which the lowliness of her birth seemed to have excluded her, but of which she was worthy, by the nobleness of her character and the purity of her mind. You know that you had continual reasons to rejoice in the selection you had made. Her gentleness, her obliging disposition, and her affection for you, equalled the charms of her person. But you did not long enjoy the happiness of beholding her. After she had made you the father of Beauty you were under the necessity of travelling to the frontiers of your Kingdom, to suppress some revolutionary demonstrations of which you had received intimation.

"During this period, you lost your dear wife, an affliction which you felt the more sensibly because, in addition to the love with which her beauty had inspired you, you had the greatest respect for the many rare qualities that adorned her mind. Despite her youth and the little education she had received, you found her naturally endowed with profound judgment, and your wisest ministers were astonished at the excellent advice she gave you, and the policy by which she enabled you to succeed in all your undertakings."

The King, who still brooded over his affliction, and to whose imagination the death of that dear wife was ever present, could not listen to this account without being sensibly affected, and the Fairy, who observed his emotion, said, "Your feelings prove that you deserved that happiness. I will no longer dwell on a subject that is so painful to you, but I must reveal to you that the supposed shepherdess was a Fairy, and my sister, who, having heard that the Fortunate Island was a charming country, and also much praise of its laws and of the gentle nature of your government, was particularly anxious to visit it.

"The dress of a shepherdess was the only disguise she assumed, intending to enjoy for a short time a pastoral life. You encountered her in her new abode. Her youth and beauty touched your heart. She yielded to a desire to discover whether the qualities of your mind equalled those she found in your person. She trusted to her condition and power as a Fairy, which could place her at a wish beyond the reach of your assiduities if they became too importunate, or if you should presume to take advantage of the humble position in which you found her.

"She was not alarmed at the sentiments with which you might inspire her, and persuaded that her virtue was sufficient to guarantee her against the snares of love, she attributed her sensations to a simple curiosity to ascertain if there were still upon the earth men capable of loving virtue unembellished by exterior ornaments, which render it more brilliant and respectable to vulgar souls than its own intrinsic merit, and frequently, by their fatal attractions, obtain the reputation of virtue for the most abominable vices.

"Under this illusion, far from retreating to our common asylum, as she had at first proposed, she chose to inhabit a little cottage she had raised for herself in the solitude in which you met her, accompanied by a phantom, representing her mother. These two persons appeared to live there upon the produce of a pretended flock that had no fear of the wolves, being, in fact, Fairies in that form. It was in that cottage she received your attentions, which produced all the effect you could desire. She could not resist the offer you made her of your crown. You now know the extent of the obligations you were under to her at a time when you imagined she owed everything to you, and were satisfied to remain in that error.

"What I now tell you is a positive proof that ambition had no share in the consent she accorded to your wishes. You are aware that we look upon the greatest Kingdoms but as gifts which we can bestow on any one at our pleasure. But she appreciated your generous behaviour, and esteeming herself happy in uniting herself to so excellent a man, she rashly entered into that engagement without reflecting on the danger which she thereby incurred.

"For our laws expressly forbid our union with those who have not as much power as ourselves, more especially when we have not arrived at that age when we are privileged to exercise our authority over others, and enjoy the right of presiding in our turn. Previous to that time we are subordinate to our elders, and that we may not abuse our power, we have only the liberty of disposing of our hands in favour of some spirit or sage whose knowledge is at least equal to our own. It is true that after that period, we are free to form what alliance we please; but it is seldom that we avail ourselves of that right and never without scandal to our order.

"Those who do are generally old Fairies, who almost always pay dearly for their folly; for they marry young men, who despise them, and, although they are not punished as criminals, they are sufficiently punished by the bad conduct of their husbands, on whom they are not permitted to avenge themselves. It is the only penalty imposed upon them. The disagreements which almost invariably follow the indiscretion they have committed takes from them the desire of revealing to those profane persons from whom they expected respect and attention the great secrets of art.

"My sister, however, was not placed in either of these positions. Endowed with every charm that could inspire affection, she was not of the required age; but she consulted only her love. She flattered herself she could keep her marriage a secret. She succeeded in so doing for a short time. We rarely make inquiries about those who are absent. Each is occupied with her own affairs, and we fly through the world, doing good or ill, according to our inclinations, without being obliged at our return to account for our actions, unless we have been guilty of some act which causes us to be talked about, or that some beneficent Fairy, moved by the unjust persecution of some unfortunate mortal, lays a complaint against the offender.

"In short, there must arise some unforeseen event to occasion us to consult the general book in which all we do is written at the same instant without the aid of hands. Saving these occasions, we have only to appear in the general assembly three times in the year; and, as we travel very swiftly, the affair does not occupy more than a couple of hours.

"My sister was obliged to give light to the throne (such is our phrase for the performance of that duty). On such occasions, she arranged for you a hunting party at some distance, or a journey of pleasure, and after your departure she feigned some indisposition, to remain alone in her cabinet, or that she had letters to write, or that she wished to repose. Neither in the palace nor amongst us was there any suspicion of that which it was so much her interest to conceal. This mystery, however, was not one for me. The consequences were dangerous, and I warned her of them, but she loved you too much to repent the step she had taken. Desiring even to justify it in my eyes, she insisted that I should pay you a visit.

"Without flattering you, I confess that, if the sight of you did not compel me entirely to excuse her weakness, it at least diminished considerably my surprise at it, and increased the zeal with which I laboured to keep it a secret. Her dissimulation was successful for two years; but at length she betrayed herself. We are obliged to confer a certain number of favours on the world generally, and to return an account of them. When my sister gave in hers, it appeared that she had limited her excursions and her benefits to the confines of the Fortunate Island.

"Several of our ill-natured Fairies blamed this conduct, and our Queen, in consequence, demanded of her why she had restricted her benevolence to this small corner of the earth, when she could not be ignorant that a young Fairy was bound to travel far and wide, and manifest to the universe at large our pleasure and our power.

"As this was no new regulation, my sister could not murmur at the enforcement of it, nor find a pretext for objecting to obey it. She promised, therefore, to do so; but her impatience to see you again, the fear of her absence being discovered at the Palace, the impossibility of acting secretly on a throne, did not permit her to absent herself long enough and often enough to fulfil her promise; and at the next assembly she could hardly prove that she had been out of the Fortunate Island for a quarter of an hour.

"Our Queen, greatly displeased with her, threatened to destroy that island, and so prevent her continuing to violate our laws. This threat agitated her so greatly that the least sharp-sighted Fairy could see to what a point she carried her interest for that fatal island, and the wicked Fairy who turned the Prince here present into a frightful Beast, was convinced by her confusion that, on opening the great book, she should find in it an important entry which would afford some exercise to her propensities for mischief. 'It is there,' she exclaimed, 'that the truth will appear, and that we shall learn what has really been her occupation!' and with these words, she opened the volume before the whole assembly, and read the details of all that had taken place during the last two years in a loud and distinct voice.

"All the Fairies made an extraordinary uproar on hearing of this degrading alliance, and overwhelmed my wretched sister with the cruellest reproaches. She was degraded from our order, and condemned to remain a prisoner amongst us. If her punishment had consisted of the first penalty only, she would have consoled herself; but the second sentence, far more terrible, made her feel all the rigour of both.

"The loss of her dignity little affected her; but, loving you fondly, she begged, with tears in her eyes, that they would be satisfied with degrading her, and not deprive her of the pleasure of living as a simple mortal with her husband and her dear daughter. Her tears and supplications touched the hearts of the younger judges, and I felt, from the murmur that arose, that if the votes had been collected at that instant, she would certainly have escaped with a reprimand.

"But one of the eldest, who, from her extreme decrepitude had obtained amongst us the name of 'the Mother of the Seasons,' did not give the Queen time to speak and admit that pity had touched her heart as well as the others. "There is no excuse for this crime,' cried the detestable old creature, in her cracked voice. 'If it is permitted to go unpunished, we shall be daily exposed to similar insults. The honour of our order is absolutely involved in it. This miserable being, attached to earth, does not regret the loss of a rank which elevated her a hundred degrees higher above monarchs than they are above their subjects. She tells us that her affections, her fears, and her wishes, all turn upon her unworthy family. It is through them we must punish her. Let her husband deplore her! Let her daughter, the shameful fruit of her illegal marriage, become the bride of a Beast, to expiate the folly of a mother who could allow herself to be captivated by the frail and contemptible beauty of a mortal!'

"This cruel speech revived the severity of many who had been previously inclined to mercy. Those who continued to pity her being too few to offer any opposition, the sentence was approved of in its integrity; and our Queen herself, whose features had indicated a feeling of compassion, resuming their severity, confirmed the majority of votes in favour of the motion of the ill-natured old Fairy. My sister, however, in her endeavours to obtain a revocation of this cruel decree, to propitiate her judges, and to excuse her marriage, had drawn so charming a portrait of you that it inflamed the heart of the Fairy Governess of the Prince (she who had opened the great volume); but this dawning passion only served to increase the hatred which that wicked Fairy already bore to your unfortunate wife.

"Unable to resist her desire to see you, she concealed her passion under the colour of a pretext that she was anxious to ascertain if you deserved that a Fairy should make such a sacrifice for you as my sister had done. As she had obtained the sanction of the assembly to her guardianship of the Prince, she could not have ventured to quit him for any length of time if the ingenuity of love had not inspired her with the idea of placing a protecting genius and two inferior and invisible Fairies to watch over him in her absence.

"After taking this precaution, there was nothing to prevent her following her inclination, which speedily carried her to the Fortunate Island. In the meanwhile, the women and officers of the imprisoned Queen, surprised that she did not come out of her private cabinet, became alarmed. The express orders she had given them not to disturb her, induced them to pass the night without knocking at the door; but impatience at last taking place of all other considerations, they knocked loudly, and no one answering, they forced the doors, under the impression that some accident had happened to her.

"Although they had prepared themselves for the worst, they were not the less astonished at perceiving no trace of her. They called her; they hunted for her in vain. They could discover nothing to appease the despair into which her disappearance had plunged them. They imagined a thousand reasons for it, each more absurd than the other. They could not suspect her evasion to be voluntary. She was all-powerful in your Kingdom. The sovereign jurisdiction you had confided to her was not disputed by any one. Everybody obeyed her cheerfully. The affection you had for each other, that which she entertained for her daughter and for her subjects, who adored her, prevented them from supposing she had fled. Where could she go to be happier? On the other hand, what man would have dared to carry off a Queen from the midst of her own guards, and the centre of her own palace? Such a ravisher must have left some indications of the road he had taken.

"The disaster was certain, although the causes of it were unknown. There was another evil to dread; namely, the feelings with which you would receive this fatal news. The innocence of those who were responsible for the safety of the Queen's person by no means satisfied them that they should not feel the effects of your wrath. They felt they must either flee the Kingdom - and thereby appear guilty of a crime they had not committed - or they must find some means of hiding this misfortune from you.

"After long deliberation, they could imagine no other than that of persuading you the Queen was dead, and this plan they put instantly into execution. They sent off a courier to inform you that she had been suddenly taken ill; a second followed a few hours afterwards, bearing the news of her death, in order to prevent your love inducing you to return post-haste to Court. Your appearance would have deranged all the measures they had taken for general security. They paid to the supposed defunct all the funeral honours due to her rank, to your affection, and the sorrow of a people who adored her, and who wept her loss as sincerely as yourself.

"This cruel adventure was always kept a profound secret from you, although it was known to every other inhabitant of the Fortunate Island. The first astonishment had given publicity to the whole affair. The affliction you felt at this loss was proportionate to your love; you found no consolation except in the innocent caresses of your infant daughter, whom you sent for to be with you. You determined never again to be separated from her; she was charming, and presented you continually with a living portrait of the Queen, her mother.

"The hostile Fairy, who had been the original cause of all this trouble by opening the great book in which she discovered my sister's marriage, had not come to see you without paying the price of her curiosity. Your appearance had produced the same effect upon her heart as it had previously done on that of your wife, and, instead of this experience inducing her to excuse my sister, she ardently desired to commit the same fault. Hovering about you invisibly, she could not resolve to quit you.

"Beholding you inconsolable, she had no hope of success, and fearing to add the shame of your refusal to the pain of disappointment, she did not dare make herself known to you; on the other hand, supposing she did appear, she imagined that by skilful manoeuvring, she might accustom you to see her, and perhaps in time induce you to love her. But to affect this she must be introduced to you; and after much pondering to find some decorous way of presenting herself, she hit on one.

"There was a neighbouring Queen who had been driven out of her dominions by a usurper, who had murdered her husband. This unhappy Princess was ranging the world to find an asylum and an avenger. The Fairy carried her off, and having deposited her in a safe place, put her to sleep, and assumed her form.

"You beheld, Sire, that disguised Fairy fling herself at your feet, and implore your protection and assistance to punish the assassin of a husband whom she professed she regretted as deeply as you did your Queen. She protested that her love for him alone impelled her to this course, and that she renounced, with all her heart, a crown which she offered to him who should avenge her dear husband.

"The unhappy pity each other. You interested yourself in her misfortunes the more readily for that she wept the loss of a beloved spouse, and that mingling her tears with yours, she talked to you incessantly of the Queen. You gave her your protection, and lost no time in re-establishing her authority in the Kingdom she pretended to, by punishing the rebels and the usurper she seemed to desire; but she would neither return to it nor quit you. She implored you, for her own security, to govern the Kingdom in her name, as you were too generous to accept it as a gift from her, and to permit her to reside at your Court.

"You could not refuse her this new favour. She appeared to be necessary to you for the education of your daughter, for the cunning Fairy knew well enough that child was the sole object of your affection. She feigned an exceeding fondness for her, and had her continually in her arms. Anticipating the request you were about to make to her, she earnestly begged to be permitted to take charge of her education, saying that she would have no heir but that dear child, whom she looked on as her own, and who was the only being she loved in the world; because she said she reminded her of a daughter she had had by her husband, and who perished along with him.

"The proposal appeared to you so advantageous that you did not hesitate to entrust the Princess to her care, and to give her full authority over her. She acquitted herself of her duties to perfection, and by her talent and her affection obtained your implicit confidence and your love as for a tender sister. This was not sufficient for her - all her anxiety was but to become your wife.

"She neglected nothing to gain this end; but even had you never been the husband of the most beautiful of Fairies, she was not formed to inspire you with love. The shape she had assumed could not bear comparison with hers into whose place she would have stolen. It was extremely ugly, and being naturally so herself, she had only the power of appearing beautiful one day in the year.

"The knowledge of this discouraging fact convinced her that to succeed she must have recourse to other charms than those of beauty. She intrigued secretly to oblige the people and the nobility to petition you to take another wife, and to point her out to you as the desirable person; but certain ambiguous conversations she had held with you, in order to sound your inclinations, enabled you easily to discover the origin of the pressing solicitations with which you were importuned.

"You declared positively that you would not hear of giving a stepmother to your daughter, nor lower her position, by making her subordinate to a Queen, from that which she held as the highest person next to yourself in the Kingdom, and the acknowledged heir to your throne. You also gave the false Queen to understand that you should feel obliged by her returning to her own dominions immediately, and without ado, and promised her that when she was settled there you would render her all the services she could expect from a faithful friend and a generous neighbour; but you did not conceal from her that if she did not take this course willingly, she ran the risk of being compelled to do so.

"The invincible obstacle you then opposed to her love threw her into a terrific rage, but she affected so much indifference about the matter that she succeeded in persuading you that her attempt was caused by ambition, and the fear that eventually you might take possession of her dominions, preferring, notwithstanding the earnestness with which she had appeared to offer them to you, to let you believe she was insincere in that case, rather than you should suspect her real sentiments. Her fury was not less violent because it was suppressed.

"Not doubting that it was Beauty who, more powerful in your heart than policy, caused you to reject the opportunity of increasing your empire in so glorious a manner, she conceived for her a hatred as violent as that which she felt for your wife, and resolved to get rid of her, fully believing that if she were dead, your subjects, renewing their remonstrance, would compel you to change your state, in order to leave a successor to the throne. The good soul was anything but of an age to present you with one; but that she cared little about. The Queen, whose resemblance she had assumed, was still young enough to have many children, and her ugliness was no obstacle to a royal and political alliance.

"Notwithstanding the official declaration you had made, it

was thought that if your daughter died you would yield to the continual representations of your council. It was believed, also, that your choice would fall upon this pretended Queen; and that idea surrounded her with numberless parasites. It was her design, therefore, by the aid of one of her flatterers, whose wife was as base as her husband, and as wicked as she was herself, to make away with your daughter. She had appointed this woman governess to the little Princess.

"These wretches settled between them that they would smother her, and report that she had died suddenly; but for more security, they decided to commit this murder in the neighbouring forest, so that nobody could surprise them in the execution of this barbarous deed. They counted on no one having the slightest knowledge of it, and that it would be impossible to blame them for not having sought for assistance before she expired, having the legitimate excuse that they were too far away from any. The husband of the governess proposed to go in search of aid as soon as the child was dead; and that no suspicion might be awakened, he was to appear surprised at finding it too late when he returned to the spot where he had left this tender victim of their fury, and he also rehearsed the sorrow and consternation he was to affect.

"When my wretched sister saw herself deprived of her power and condemned to a cruel imprisonment, she requested me to console you and to watch over the safety of her child. It was unnecessary for her to take that precaution. The tie which unites us, and the pity I felt for her, would have sufficed to ensure you my protection, and her entreaties could not increase the zeal with which I hastened to fulfil her decrees.

"I saw you as often as I could, and as much as prudence permitted me, without incurring the risk of arousing the suspicions of our enemy, who would have denounced me as a

Fairy in whom sisterly affection prevailed over the honour of her order, and who protected a guilty race. I neglected nothing to convince all the Fairies that I had abandoned my sister to her unhappy fate, and, by so doing, trusted to be more at liberty to serve her.

"As I watched every movement of your perfidious admirer, not only with my own eyes, but those of the Genii, who were my servants, her horrible intentions were not unknown to me. I could not oppose her by open force; and though it would have been easy for me to annihilate those into whose hands she had delivered the little innocent, prudence restrained me; for, had I carried off your daughter, the malignant Fairy would have retaken her from me, without its being possible for me to defend her.

"It is a law amongst us that we must be a thousand years old before we can dispute the power of the ancient Fairies, or at any rate we must have become serpents. The perils which accompany the latter condition cause us to call it the Terrible Act. The bravest amongst us shudder at the thought of undertaking it. We hesitate a long time before we can resolve to expose ourselves to its consequences; and without the urgent motive of hatred, love, or vengeance, there are few who do not prefer waiting for time to make them Elders than to acquire their privilege by that dangerous transformation, in which the greater number are destroyed.

"I was in this position. I wanted ten years of the thousand, and I had no resource but in artifice. I employed it successfully. I took the form of a monstrous she-bear, and, hiding myself in the forest selected for the execution of this detestable deed, when the wretches arrived to fulfil the barbarous order they had received, I flung myself upon the woman who had the child in her arms, and who had already placed her hand on its mouth. Her fright made her drop the precious burden, but she was not allowed to escape so easily; the horror I felt at her unnatural conduct inspired me with the ferocity of the brute I had assumed the form of.

"I strangled her, as well as the traitor who accompanied her, and I carried off Beauty, after having rapidly stripped off her clothes and dyed them with the blood of her enemies. I scattered them also about the forest, taking the precaution to tear them in several places, so that they should not suspect the Princess had escaped; and I withdrew, delighted at having succeeded so completely.

"The Fairy believed her object had been attained. The death of her two accomplices was an advantage to her. She was mistress of her secret, and the fate they had met with was but what she had herself destined them to, in recompense of their guilty services. Another circumstance was also favourable to her. Some shepherds who had seen this affair from a distance ran for assistance, which arrived just in time to see the infamous wretches expire, and prevent the possibility of suspicion that she had any part in it.

"The same circumstances were equally favourable to my enterprise. The wicked Fairy was as fully convinced as the people by them. The event was so natural, that she never doubted it. She did not even condescend to exert her skill to satisfy herself of the fact. I was delighted at her fancied security. I should not have been the strongest had she attempted to recover little Beauty, because, in addition to the reasons which made her my superior, and which I have explained to you, she possessed the advantage of having received that child from you. You had deputed to her your authority, which you alone could re-assume, and short of your wresting her yourself out of her hands, nothing could interfere with the control she had a right to exercise over the Princess till she was married.

"Preserved from this anxiety, I found myself overwhelmed by another, on recollecting that the Mother of the Seasons had condemned my niece to marry a Beast; but she was then not three years old, and I flattered myself I should be able, by study, to discover some expedient to prevent this curse being fulfilled to the letter, and to evade it by some equivocation. I had plenty of time to ponder on it, and my first care was, therefore, only to find some spot where I could place my precious charge in safety.

"Profound secrecy was absolutely necessary to me. I dared not place her in a palace, nor exercise for her benefit any of the magnificent wonders of our art. Our enemy would have noticed it. It would have awakened an anxiety, the consequences of which would have been fatal to us. I thought it better to assume a humble garb, and confide the infant to the care of the first person I met with, who appeared to me to be an honest man, and under whose roof I could promise myself she would enjoy the comforts of life.

"Chance soon favoured my intentions. I found what suited me exactly. It was a small house in a village, the door of which was open. I entered this cottage, which appeared to me that of a peasant in easy circumstances. I saw by the light of a lamp three country women asleep beside a cradle, which I concluded contained a baby. The cradle did not at all correspond with the general simplicity of the apartment. Everything about it was sumptuous.

"I imagined that its little occupant was ill, and that the deep sleep into which its nurses had fallen was the consequence of long watching over it. I approached silently, with the intention of curing the infant, and anticipated with pleasure the surprise of these women, on awaking, to find their invalid restored to health, without knowing what to attribute it to. I was about to take the child out of the cradle in order to breathe health into it; but my good intentions were vain - it expired at the instant I touched it.

"I immediately conceived the idea of taking advantage of this melancholy event, and substituting my niece for the dead child, which, by good fortune, was also a girl. I lost no time in making the exchange, and bearing away the lifeless infant, buried it carefully. I then returned to the house, at the door of which I knocked long and loudly, to awaken them.

"I told them, feigning a provincial dialect, that I was a stranger to those parts, who was in want of a night's lodging. They good-naturedly offered me one, and then went to look at their nursling, whom they found quietly asleep, with all the appearance of being in perfect health. They were astonished and delighted, not dreaming of the deception I had practised upon them. They informed me that the child was the daughter of a rich merchant; that one of their party had been her nurse, and after having weaned her had restored her to her parents, but that the child, having fallen ill in her father's house, had been sent back to the country, in hope that the change of air would be of service to her.

"They added, with satisfied countenances, that the experiment had succeeded, and produced a better effect than all the remedies which had been resorted to previous to its adoption. They determined to carry her back to her father as soon as it was daylight, in order to afford him, as early as possible, the gratification he would derive from her restoration, for conducing to which, also, they expected to receive a liberal reward, as the child was his particular favourite, although the youngest of eleven.

"At sunrise they set out, and I feigned to continue my journey, congratulating myself on having so well provided for my niece's safety. To insure this object more completely, and induce the supposed father still more to attach himself to the little girl, I assumed the form of one of those women who go about telling fortunes, and arriving at the merchant's door just as the nurses reached it with the child, I followed them into the house.

"He received them with delight, and taking the little girl in his arms, became the dupe of his paternal affection, and fancied that the emotions simply caused by his kindly disposition were the mysterious workings of nature at the sight of his offspring. I seized this opportunity of increasing the interest he believed he had in the child. 'Look well upon this little one, my good gentleman,' said I, in the usual language of the class to which by my dress I appeared to belong. 'She will be a great honour to your family, she will bring you immense wealth, and save your life and that of all your children. She will be so beautiful that she will be called Beauty by all who behold her.'

"As a reward for my prediction, he gave me a piece of gold, and I withdrew, perfectly satisfied. I had no longer any reason for residing with the race of Adam. To profit by my leisure, I returned to Fairyland, resolving to remain in it some time. I passed my days there quietly in consoling my sister, in giving her news of her dear daughter, and in assuring her that, far from forgetting her, you cherished her memory as fondly as you had formerly herself.

"Such, great King, was our situation whilst you were suffering under the fresh calamity which had deprived you of your child, and renewed the affliction you had felt at the loss of her mother. Although you could not positively accuse the person to whom you had confided the infant of being the wilful cause of the accident, it was still impossible for you not to look upon her with an evil eye; for though it did not appear that she was guilty of intentional mischief, it was certainly through her neglecting to see that the young Princess was properly attended and protected that the event had proved fatal.

"After the first paroxysms of your grief had subsided, she flattered herself that no obstacle would arise to prevent your espousing her. She caused her emissaries to renew the proposal to you; but she was undeceived, and her mortification was excessive, when you declared that not only were your intentions unchanged respecting a second marriage, but that even, could anything alter your determination, it would never be in her favour. To this declaration you added a positive order for her to quit the Kingdom immediately. Her presence continually reminded you of your child, and renewed your affliction. Such was the reason you adduced for this step; but your principal object was to put an end to the intrigues she was constantly carrying on in order to gain her end.

"She was furious; but she was obliged to obey without being able to avenge herself. I had persuaded one of our ancient Fairies to protect you. Her power was considerable, for she joined to her age the advantage of having been four times a serpent. In proportion to the excessive peril incurred by that process, are the honours and powers attached to it. This Fairy, out of consideration for me, took you under her protection, and put it out of the power of your indignant lover to do you any mischief.

"This disappointment was fortunate for the Queen, whose form she had assumed. She awoke her from her magic slumber, and concealing from her the criminal use she had made of her features, placed her conduct in the best light before her.

"She expatiated on the value of her intercession with the King, and on the trouble she had saved her, and gave her the best advice she could how to maintain herself for the future in her proper person. It was then that, to console herself for your indifference, the Fairy returned to the young Prince and resumed her care of him. She became too fond of him, and not being able to make herself beloved, she caused him to suffer that terrible effect of her fury.

"In the meanwhile, I had insensibly arrived at the privileged age, and my power was increased, but my desire to serve my sister and yourself induced me to feel that still I had not sufficient. My sincere friendship blinding me to the perils of "the Terrible Act," I resolved to undertake it.

"I became a serpent, and passed fortunately through the ordeal. I was then in a position to act openly in favour of those who were persecuted by my malicious companions. If I cannot at all times entirely dissolve their fatal spells, I can at least counteract them by my skill and by my counsels.

"My niece was amongst the number of those whom I could not completely favour. Not daring to discover all the interest I took in her, it appeared to me that the best thing I could do was to allow her still to pass as the merchant's daughter. I visited her under various forms, and always returned satisfied. Her virtue and beauty equalled her good sense. At the age of fourteen, she had already given proof of great fortitude during the changes of fortune which had befallen her supposed father.

"I was delighted to find that the cruellest reverses had not been able to affect her tranquillity. On the contrary, by her cheerfulness, by the charm of her conversation, she had succeeded in restoring it to the hearts of her father and her brothers; and I rejoiced to observe also that her sentiments were worthy of her birth. These pleasant reflections were, however, mingled with much bitterness, when I remembered that, with so many perfections, she was destined to be the wife of a Beast. I toiled, I studied night and day to find some means of saving her from so great a misfortune, and was in despair at finding none.

"This anxiety did not prevent me, however, from paying occasional visits to you. Your wife, who was deprived of that liberty, implored me incessantly to go and see you; and, notwithstanding the protection of our friend, her affectionate heart was continually alarmed about you, and persuaded her that the instant I lost sight of you would be the last of your life, and in which you would be sacrificed to the fury of our enemy. This fear possessed her so strongly, that she scarcely gave me a moment's rest. No sooner did I bring her news of you, than she supplicated me so earnestly to return to you, that it was impossible to refuse her.

"Compassionating her anxiety, and more desirous to end it than to save myself the trouble it gave me, I employed against my cruel companion the same weapons she had made use of against you. I proceeded to open the great book. By good fortune, it was at the very moment she was holding that conversation with the Queen and Prince which terminated in his transformation. I lost not a word of it, and my rapture was extreme at finding that, in seeking to assure her vengeance, she neutralized, without knowing it, the mischief which the Mother of the Seasons had done us in dooming Beauty to be the bride of a Beast.

"To crown our happiness, she added conditions so

advantageous, that it almost seemed as if she made them on purpose to oblige me, for she thereby furnished my sister's daughter with an opportunity of proving that she was worthy of being the issue of the purest of Fairy-blood.

"The slightest sign or gesture expresses amongst us as much as it would take an ordinary mortal three days to explain. I uttered but one contemptuous word. It was enough to inform the assembly that our enemy had pronounced her own sentence in that which she had caused ten years before to be passed upon your wife.

"At the age of the latter, the weakness of love was more natural than at the advanced period of existence of a Fairy of the highest order. I spoke of the base and wicked actions which had accompanied that superannuated passion. I urged that if so many infamous acts were allowed to pass unpunished, mortals would be justified in saying that Fairies existed in the world but to dishonour nature and afflict the human race. Presenting the book to them, I condensed this abrupt oration in the single word, 'Behold!'. It was not the less powerful in its effect.

"There were present also friends of mine, both young and old, who treated the amorous fairy as she deserved. She had not succeeded in becoming your wife, and to that disgrace was now added degradation from her order, and imprisonment, as in the case of the Queen of the Fortunate Island.

"This council was held whilst she was with you, Madam, and your son. As soon as she appeared amongst us, the result was communicated to her. I had the pleasure to be present, after which, closing the book, I descended rapidly from the middle region of air in which our Empire is situated, to combat the effect of the despair to which you were ready to abandon yourselves. I performed my journey in as short a space of time as I had occupied with my laconical address. I arrived soon enough to promise you my assistance. All sorts of reasons combined to invite me.

"Your virtues, your misfortunes," said the Fairy, turning to the Prince, "the advantages they offered to Beauty made me see in you the Beast that suited me. You appeared to me worthy of each other, and I felt convinced that when you became acquainted, your hearts would do each other mutual justice.

"You know," she continued, addressing the Queen, "what I have since done to attain my object, and by what means I obliged Beauty to come to this Palace, where the sight of the Prince, and her interviews with him, in the dreams I conjured up for her, had the effect I desired. They kindled love in her heart without diminishing her virtue or weakening the sense of duty and gratitude which attached her to the Beast. In short, I have happily brought my scheme to perfection.

"Yes, Prince," pursued the Fairy, "you have no longer anything to fear from your enemy. She is stripped of her power, and will never again be able to injure you by other spells. You have exactly fulfilled the conditions she imposed on you. Had you not done so, you would have been still bound by them, notwithstanding her eternal degradation. You have made yourself beloved without the aid of your rank or your intelligence; and you, Beauty, are equally relieved from the curse pronounced upon you by the Mother of the Seasons. You cheerfully accepted a Beast for your husband. She has nothing more to exact. All now tends to your happiness."

The Fairy ceased speaking, and the King threw himself at her feet. "Great Fairy," he exclaimed, "how can I thank you for all the favours you have heaped on my family? My gratitude for the benefits you have bestowed on us far exceeds my power of expression; but, my august sister," he added, "that title encourages me to ask more favours; for, despite the obligations I am already under to you, I cannot avoid confessing to you that I shall never be truly happy so long as I am deprived of the presence of my beloved Fairy Queen. This account of what she has done and what she has suffered for me would increase my love and my affliction, were either of them capable of being augmented. Ah, Madam," he added, "can you not crown all your benefactions by enabling me to behold her?"

The question was useless. If the Fairy had had the power to have afforded him that gratification, she was too willing to have waited for the request; but she could not alter what the Council of the Fairies had decreed. The young Queen being a prisoner in the middle regions of air, there was not the shadow of a chance of his being enabled to see her; and the Fairy was about to explain this to him kindly, and to exhort him to await patiently some unforeseen events, of which she might take advantage, when an enchanting melody stole upon their ears and interrupted her.

The King, his daughter, the Queen, and the Prince, were in ecstasies, but the Fairy experienced another sort of surprise. Such music indicated the triumph of some Fairy. She could not imagine what Fairy had achieved a victory. Her fears suggested that it was the old one, or the Mother of the Seasons, who in her absence had obtained, the former her liberty, or the latter permission to persecute the lovers afresh.

She was in this perplexity when it was agreeably ended by the presence of her Fairy-sister, the Queen of the Fortunate Island, who suddenly appeared in the centre of that charming group. She was no less lovely than when the King, her husband, lost her. The monarch, who instantly recognised her, making the respect he owed her yield to the love he had cherished for her, embraced her with such transports of joy, that the Queen herself was surprised at them.

The Fairy, her sister, could not imagine to what fortunate miracle she was indebted for her liberty; but the royal Fairy informed her that she owed her happiness solely to her own courage, which had impelled her to hazard her own existence to preserve another's. "You are aware," said she to the Fairy, "that the daughter of our Queen was received into the order at her birth; that her father was not a sublunary being, but the sage, Amadabak, whose alliance is an honour to the Fairy race, and whose sublime knowledge invests him with much higher powers. Notwithstanding this, however, it was imperative for his daughter to become a serpent at the end of her first hundred years.

"The fatal period arrived, and our Queen, as tender a mother, and as anxious respecting the fate of this dear infant as any ordinary parent could be, could not resolve to expose her to the many chances of destruction in that shape, the misfortunes of those who had perished being but too notorious for her not to feel the greatest alarm.

"My wretched situation depriving me of all hope of again beholding my affectionate husband and my lovely daughter, I had conceived a perfect disgust for a life which I was doomed to pass apart from them. Without the least hesitation, therefore, I offered to become a crawling reptile in the place of the young Fairy. I saw with delight a certain, prompt, and honourable mode of delivering myself from all the miseries with which I was overwhelmed, by death or by a glorious emancipation, which would render me mistress of my own actions, and thereby enable me to rejoin my husband.

"Our Queen hesitated as little to accept this offer, so gratifying to her maternal affection, as I did to make it. She embraced me a hundred times, and promised to restore me to liberty unconditionally, and re-establish me in all my privileges, if I was fortunate enough to pass unharmed through that perilous enterprise. I did do so, and the fruit of my labours was enjoyed by the young Fairy, for whom I had been the substitute.

"The success of my first trial encouraged me to make a second for my own benefit. I underwent the transformation anew, and was equally fortunate. This last act made me an Elder, and, consequently, independent. I was not long in profiting by my liberty, and flying here to rejoin a family so dear to me."

As soon as the Fairy had finished her narrative, the embraces were renewed by her affectionate auditors. It was a charming confusion, in which each caressed the other almost without knowing what they were about: Beauty, particularly, enchanted at appertaining to such an illustrious family, and no longer fearing to degrade the Prince, her cousin, by causing him to form an alliance beneath him.

CHAPTER XI
MARRIAGE GUESTS

Although transported by the excess of her happiness, Beauty did not forget the worthy man whom she had formerly believed to be her father. She recalled to her Fairy aunt the promise she had made to her, that he and his children should have the honour of being present at her marriage. She was still speaking to her on this subject when they saw from the window sixteen persons on horseback, most of whom had hunting-horns, and appeared in considerable confusion. Their disorder evidently arose from their horses having ran away with them. Beauty instantly recognised them as the six sons of the worthy merchant, the five daughters, and their five lovers.

Everybody but the Fairy was surprised at this abrupt entrance. Those who made it were not less so, at finding themselves carried by the speed of their unmanageable horses into a palace totally unknown to them.

This is the way it happened. They were all out hunting, when their horses, suddenly uniting themselves as in one squadron, galloped off with them at such speed to the Palace that all their efforts to stop them were perfectly useless.

Beauty, thoughtless of her present dignity, hastened to receive and reassure them. She embraced them all kindly. The good man himself next appeared, but not in the same disorder.

A horse had neighed and scratched at his door. He had no doubt that it came to seek him by order of his dear daughter. He mounted him without fear, and, perfectly satisfied as to whether the steed would bear him, he was not at all surprised to find himself in the courtyard of a Palace which he now saw for the third time, and to which he felt convinced he had been conducted to witness the marriage of Beauty and the Beast.

The moment he perceived her, he ran to her with open arms, blessing the happy moment that presented her again to his sight, and heaping benedictions on the generous Beast who had permitted him to return; he looked about for him in every direction, to offer him his most humble thanks for all the favours he had heaped on his family, and particularly on his youngest daughter. He was vexed at not seeing him and began to apprehend that his conjectures were erroneous.

Still, the presence of all his children seemed to support the idea he had formed, as they would scarcely have been all assembled in that spot if some solemn ceremony, such as that marriage, were not to be celebrated. These reflections, which the good man made to himself, did not prevent him from pressing Beauty fondly in his arms, and bathing her cheek with tears of joy.

After allowing due time for this first expression of his feelings, "Enough, good man," said the Fairy. "You have sufficiently caressed this Princess. It is time that, ceasing to regard her as a father, you should learn that that title does not appertain to you, and that you must now do her homage as your sovereign. She is the Princess of the Fortunate Island, daughter of the King and Queen whom you see before you. She is about to become the wife of this Prince. Here stands the Prince's mother, sister of the King. I am a Fairy, her friend, and the aunt of Beauty. As to the Prince," added the Fairy, observing the expression of the good man's face, "he is better known to you than you imagine; but he is much altered since you last saw him. In a word, he was the Beast himself."

The father and his sons were enchanted at these wonderful tidings, while the sisters felt a painful jealousy, but they endeavoured to conceal it under the mask of a gratification, which deceived no one. The others, however, feigned to believe them sincere. As to the lovers, who had been rendered inconstant by the hope of possessing Beauty, and who had only returned to their first attachments on their despairing to obtain her, they knew not what to think.

The merchant could not help weeping, without being able to tell whether his tears were caused by the pleasure of seeing the happiness of Beauty, or by the sorrow of losing so perfect a daughter. His sons were agitated by similar feelings. Beauty, extremely affected by this evidence of their love, entreated those on whom she now depended, as well as the Prince, her future husband, to permit her to reward such tender attachment.

Her entreaty testified the goodness of her heart too sincerely not to be listened to. They were laden with bounties, and by permission of the King, the Prince, and the Queen, Beauty continued to call them by the tender names of father, brothers, and even sisters, though she was not ignorant that the latter were as little so in heart as they were in blood. She desired they would all, in return, call her by the name they were wont to do when they believed her to be a member of their family.

The old man and his children were appointed to offices in the Court of Beauty, and enjoyed the pleasure of living continually near her, in a station sufficiently exalted to be generally respected. The lovers of her sisters, whose passion for Beauty might easily have been revived, if they had not known it would be useless, thought themselves too happy in being united to the good man's daughters, and becoming allied to persons for whom Beauty retained so much goodwill.

All those she desired to be present at her wedding having arrived, the celebration of it was no longer delayed. The festivities lasted many days, and ended at length only because the Fairy aunt of the young bride pointed out to them the propriety of leaving that beautiful retreat, and returning to their dominions, to show themselves to their subjects.

It was quite time she should recall their Kingdom to their recollection and the indispensable duties which demanded their presence. Enraptured with the scenes around them, entranced by the pleasure of loving and expressing their love to each other, they had entirely forgotten their royal state and the cares that attend it.

The newly-married pair, indeed, proposed to the Fairy that they should abdicate, and resign their power into the hands of anyone she should select; but that wise being represented to them clearly that they were under as great an obligation to fulfil the destiny which had confided to them the government of a nation as that nation was to preserve for them an unshaken loyalty.

They yielded to these just remonstrances, but the Prince and Beauty stipulated that they should be allowed occasionally to visit that spot, and cast aside for a while the cares inseparable from their station, and that they should be waited on by the invisible Genii or the animals who had attended them during the preceding years. They availed themselves as often as possible of this liberty. Their presence seemed to embellish the spot. All were eager to please them. The Genii awaited their visits with impatience, and received them with joy, testifying in a hundred ways the delight their return afforded them.

The Fairy, whose foresight neglected nothing, gave them a chariot, drawn by twelve white stags with golden horns and hoofs, like those she drove herself. The speed of these animals was almost greater than that of thought; and, drawn by them, you could easily make the tour of the world in two hours. By this means they lost no time in travelling. They profited by every moment of leisure, and went frequently in this elegant equipage to visit her father, the King of the Fortunate Island, who had grown so young again through the return of his Fairy Queen, that he equalled in face and form the Prince, his son-in-law. He felt also equally happy, being neither less enamoured nor less eager to prove to his wife his unceasing affection, while she, on her part, responded to his love with all that tenderness which had previously been the cause of so much misfortune to her.

She had been received by her subjects with transports of joy as great as those of grief which her loss had occasioned them. She had always loved them dearly, and her will being now unfettered, she proved as much, by showering upon them for many centuries all the benefits they could desire. Her power, assisted by the friendship of the Queen of the Fairies, preserved the life, health, and youth of the King, her husband, for ages. He only ceased to exist because no mortal can live forever.

The Queen and the Fairy, her sister, were equally attentive to Beauty, her husband, the Queen, his mother, the old man, and all his family, so that there never was known people who lived so long. The Queen, mother of the Prince, caused this marvellous history to be recorded in the archives of her Kingdom and in those of the Fortunate Island, that it might be handed down to posterity. They also disseminated copies of it throughout the Universe, so that the world at large might never cease to talk of the wonderful adventures of Beauty and the Beast.

ABOUT THE AUTHOR

Gabrielle-Suzanne Barbot de Villeneuve (c. 1695 – 29 December 1755) was a French author influenced by Madame d'Aulnoy and Charles Perrault.

Madame de Villeneuve was born in La Rochelle. She is particularly noted for her *La Belle et la Bête*, which is the oldest known variant of the fairy tale *Beauty and the Beast*. First published in '*La jeune américaine, et les contes marins*', it is over a hundred pages long, containing many subplots, and involving a genuinely savage - i.e. 'stupid' - Beast, not merely a change of appearance.

Her lengthy version was abridged, rewritten, and published by Jeanne-Marie Leprince de Beaumont in 1756, to produce the version most commonly retold.

In 1767, she wrote a novel *La Jardinière de Vincennes*. She was a close friend of the controversial writer Claude Jolyot de Crébillon. She died in Paris.

Made in the USA
Middletown, DE
04 July 2015